STOWAWAY

DARCY FLYNN

Copyright 2018 by Darcy Flynn
Paper Moon Publishing
Cover Design by Rae Monet, Inc.
Book Design by Jesse Gordon

Acknowledgments

I would like to thank the wonderful volunteers at GulfQuest National Maritime Museum of the Gulf of Mexico for their warm welcome and their gift of time during my research visit.

I especially want to thank Amy Raley, GulfQuest's Education Manager for setting everything up for me and giving me the grand tour!

Thank you to Russell Taylor, retired captain and museum volunteer for thoughtfully and patiently answering all of my questions. One of the many highlights was getting first hand experience at the Take The Helm simulator where you showed me the ins and outs of navigating a cargo ship into port. Your travel experience through international waters was inspiring and your many stories about life at sea highly entertaining.

Thank you to my amazing critique partners, Cindy Brannam and Jeanne Hardt for always cheering me on. You guys know how special you are to me!

To my wonderful editor, Alicia Dean. I so enjoyed brainstorming with you about this story while in Nashville. It was such fun having you on my home turf. As always your edits are encouraging, thoughtful and with purpose.

My faithful beta readers, Amy Mauldin and Brenda Jeffries, thank you for catching those pesky typos and for loving my stories!

Last, but by no means least, thank you to Katie Puckett, my super talented, Belmont University Intern, not only for your creative meme making skills, but also for your thoughtful critique after beta reading this story. I so enjoyed working with you!

DEDICATION

My father, William Bryan Griffin, having been deserted by his father who bore the same name, was renamed *Jack*, by his granddad Hatcher. From that moment on, *everyone* called him Jack.

As I grew up, I too, came to call him Jack, my teenage friends also called him Jack, and today, his grown grandchildren…yep you got it, call him Jack. Great-grandfather Hatcher had no idea what he'd started!

My father served almost 40 years as a Sanitation Specialist for the United States Public Health Service, having spent the bulk of his career in and around major shipyards in the United States and abroad. During that time, he inspected major airlines, romantic riverboats like the *Delta Queen*, and the cargo shipping line, *Lykes Brothers Steamship Company*, with the goal of ensuring the health and well-being of passengers and crew alike. His forty years of service played a vital role in preventing the spread of communicable diseases.

As a child, I'd watch him unroll large, thick, stacks of the ship's plans across our dining room table. He'd study them the night before he was to board the vessel, where he'd spend several days covering 166 separate ship areas. At the time, the job seemed enormous and extremely complex, and then later, as an adult, I realized I was right.

Due to the nature of my story and the fact it takes place aboard a cargo ship, I wanted to give one of my character's my father's name, thus Miranda's uncle, Captain *Jack* Farthing, was born.

Love you, Jack. I miss you every day. This one's for you.

CHAPTER ONE

"You know I adore you, but I will not marry some stranger. How can you even suggest such a thing?" Miranda Merrick held each end of her father's black bow tie and evened up the edges. John Merrick stood dutifully, chin in air, while her fingers flipped and tucked the fabric into place.

"Did I say marry?" he said.

"No, but you implied it." She fought the temptation to knot the fine silk tightly around his neck.

"Is it so wrong for an aging father of an only child and heiress to the Merrick fortune to want to see his daughter settled before his demise?"

"You've certainly pulled out all the stops this time – aging father – only child – heiress."

"I know. But, seriously, I'm not getting any younger."

"Haven't you heard? Seventy's the new fifty."

"Not in my case."

"What on earth? Dad. You're as healthy as a mule."

"And no doubt acting like the back end of one, right?"

"Hey, you said it." She chuckled, but the expression on his face made her pause. "You're not joking." She folded her arms and gave him her - someday I'll command my own ship - stare. "What are you up to, *Father*?"

"Oh dear. When you use the F word, I know I'm in trouble." A twinkle filled his gray eyes.

She shook her head. "You're impossible."

"Fine. Grandchildren, then. Before I'm senile."

"How about we get through this party first. Afterward, we can discuss any and all possible suitors you have in mind for me."

She gave a last little tug on his tie. "That should do it." Placing her hands on his shoulders, she turned him toward the mirror. "What do you think?"

He grabbed both ends of the tie, tweaked it right, then left. "Nice. You inherited your mother's skill."

With a slight turn of his head, he scanned her from head to toe. "Isn't that dress one of hers?"

"You know it is."

He caught her reflection in the mirror and winked. She smiled back.

"I told you to buy a new gown for this evening."

"I know. But I love wearing her clothes."

"I can see why. That sky blue is exceptionally beautiful on you. Complements your red hair." He presented his arm. "Ready?"

"Ready." Miranda looped her hand through his bent elbow, then proceeded down the wide hallway at her father's side.

As they strolled down the long corridor, strains of classical music filtered upward from the ballroom below. Most of the guests would have arrived by now and be expecting the distinguished entrance from the host and hostess.

As they neared the grand staircase her father said, "If you would at least agree to meet the man."

She sighed. "Still harping on that, are we?" She'd hoped her father would let the subject go. But when John Merrick put his mind to something, he was like a tenacious bulldog. Most of the time she'd found his tendency to overprotect her rather sweet, but this attempt at securing a husband for her was the last straw.

"And where on earth did you find this paragon of virtue? For that's what he must be for you to believe he is my *Mr. Right.*"

"Only you can decide if he's right for you."

"Well, it's nice to know I still have a choice in the matter. I guess I should be thankful for small mercies."

"And," he cleared his throat, "what better place to meet someone new than with a houseful of guests."

Her breath caught. "You didn't."

"I merely want to introduce you. In a group setting." He waved his hand through the air. "Pretend this is like one of those matchmaking sites where people meet strangers all the time."

All she could do was gape at him. This wasn't the first time her father had made such an absurd suggestion, but to have actually invited the man to their home - without her knowledge - was inexcusable.

"After your mother died, I'd hoped your time here taking her place...being at the helm of our estate, would've lessened your desire to go to sea."

"Oh, Dad. Of course I've enjoyed being in charge of our home. I've learned so much, but no modern-day woman in her right mind would agree to an arranged marriage. Surely you can see that."

"I know." He patted her hand.

"And I do want to be at the helm... Of my own ship."

He sighed heavily, nodding. "If your heart hasn't changed after five years, then I shouldn't expect any more from you."

"Look, Dad. I'm always happy to meet any of your friends or acquaintances. But that's all I can promise. Is that clear?"

"Sometimes marriage isn't just about love. It's about family expectations."

She eyed him. "What are you saying?"

"More than I'd intended. I didn't mean to upset you."

His face settled into a weary expression she'd not seen since her mother's death. Old and worn, as if a mountain of worries had suddenly taken its toll.

As if he'd carried the entire weight of one of their cargo ships.

They paused at the top of the staircase.

"I'll explain everything, after the party," he said.

"After the party, then."

* * *

Somewhat dazed, she pasted on her shipping heiress smile and moved down the long flight of steps with the grace befitting her position. As much as she wanted to go to sea, to command her own Merrick vessel, her duties as woman of the house had not appalled her in the least. She loved hosting social gatherings, whether they were business related or for family and friends. It wasn't that she hated her life. On the contrary. Who wouldn't like being the daughter of Forbes's Entrepreneur of the Year? But the sea called to her with a lover's intensity she found hard to ignore.

Her grandfather had understood – taking her on many voyages until his death when she was eleven. Not long afterward, her Uncle Jack had invited her to join him. She loved her father dearly and complied with his wishes believing at the time they would only last a few months at most. But now, five years later, she found herself resentful - toward her father, the house, Charleston and basically frustrated with her current state.

Somewhere in her musings, the sound of applause brought her back to the present. With the grand entrance behind her, she left John Merrick's side to circulate amongst the guests.

She took a deep, settling breath, and wound her way through the ballroom, smiling and nodding toward several couples mingling nearby.

"Lovely evening," one of the women said.

"Thank you. Please enjoy yourselves." Miranda's smile encompassed the little group.

She stepped past them, her thoughts still burning within her. She didn't mean to sound ungrateful, but lately she'd become restless, even agitated, and if she didn't get back on the ocean soon, she'd burst.

For the past several years, she'd kept her feelings to herself, never letting her father know how she felt, but this talk of an arranged marriage appalled her. She loved her dad, but how could he even suggest such a thing? They were quite close and that was the problem. She'd always found it difficult saying no to him.

"Lovely party, Miranda… Miranda?"

"Oh, Mrs. Nelson. I'm so sorry." She shook her head. "I was somewhere else."

"I was just complimenting you on the gala. Your mother would've been so proud of you."

"Thank you so much."

"And I have to say the Lobster Newberg was simply divine. Please compliment your cook."

"I certainly will."

Miranda crossed the glamorous ballroom. The governor and his wife stood chatting beneath the crystal chandelier with the president of one of the local universities.

Along with Charleston's elite, the guest list read like a Who's Who of top international shipping and maritime companies from across the globe.

On her way to the kitchen, Miranda paused for a quick check at the dessert table. A selection of tortes, soufflés, and custards sat appetizingly on silver trays. She'd made most of the confections herself. It had been one of the many activities she'd shared with her mother, a pastry chef in her own right, having written several recipe books before Miranda's birth.

Satisfied, she made her way to the kitchen. As she pushed through the swinging door, the staff glanced up at her entrance.

"Everyone doing okay? Mrs. Wayne, have you taken your break yet? You know how your knee flares up when you stand too long." She paused near the stove for a quick bite to eat. "You guys need anything?"

"I could use a few more dessert trays," Mrs. Wayne said.

"I'm on it." Miranda crossed the kitchen, dabbing her mouth with a napkin, and entered the butler's pantry. She selected a variety of platters, then grabbed the door handle and pushed. Nothing. It wouldn't budge. She rolled her eyes and banged on the door with the side of her fist. Two seconds later Mrs. Wayne yanked it open.

"Are you all right? I know how you hate tight spaces."

"Yeah, I'm fine. I'm just glad someone heard me."

"I figured you might need help. Some of those platters are heavy."

The two of them carried the trays back into the kitchen and set them on the island.

"I thought Henry was having that latch repaired," Miranda said.

"That man's a bit uppity if you ask me."

"Aren't butlers supposed to be?"

Mrs. Wayne chuckled. "I suppose. But, don't you worry. I'll get someone here to take care of that lock."

As Miranda started to exit the kitchen, she glanced back. "Oh, and Mae - high marks on the Lobster Newberg from Mrs. Nelson."

"Let me guess… Outstanding?"

Miranda shook her head and struck a pose. "Simply divine."

She rejoined the party and strolled through the house looking for her father. He'd never been much on the social scene, even when her mother was alive – another reason Miranda had agreed to stay on for as long as she had.

She hadn't seen him since they'd parted at the foot of the staircase and wondered who he'd closeted himself with this time. Her Mr. Right? She groaned at the unwelcome thought and made her way to the library.

The massive wooden door stood slightly ajar. As she placed her hand on it, she overheard several deep, male voices in conversation. She recognized her father's but not the others. She leaned in and peeked through the two-inch opening.

Her father sat next to a middle-aged man wearing glasses who was unknown to her. She assumed he was a party guest as he was dressed in a dark navy suit. She couldn't see the other gentleman at all, as he was hidden behind the door out of her line of sight. Could he be the man her father wanted her to meet? She drew back, ready to leave.

"…Sabotage."

Miranda froze.

"… Adding to the financial mess the company's already in."

She leaned closer, focusing on their conversation.

"Carl, are you certain?" Her father's voice held a resigned, haunted quality she found disturbing.

"I'm sorry, but that's what it looks like." The man in the glasses spoke so low she could barely make out what he was saying.

"How could something like this have happened?" her father said. "My brother-in-law is a stickler when it comes to his crew - hand picks them. He would never hire anyone without proper credentials."

At the risk of being discovered she pressed closer to the two inch opening. Even though their voices were low and somewhat muffled, she was able to make out most of what they were saying.

"Credentials can be forged." It was the first time the man behind the door had spoken. Something in his tone raised her hackles. Was he suggesting Captain Jack was incompetent?

"Sand in the lubrication system is a deliberate act, and the fact it was added past any filters which otherwise would strain them out, can't be anything *but* sabotage," the stranger hidden behind the door continued. "And that action was the direct result of someone onboard the *Elle Merrick*."

"Whether or not there's more than one saboteur has yet to be determined," Carl said. "But it's highly unlikely that it's only one person."

"Either way, your brother-in-law needs to be replaced," the man behind the door said. "For his own safety, if nothing else. He's no longer a young man, you know."

Financial problems? Seriously? How could her father have kept this from her? And, Captain Jack... Replaced? Never. He lived and breathed the *Elle Merrick*.

As she tried to make sense of what she'd heard, Carl stood and shook hands with her father. "I'll keep you informed on my investigation." Carl headed for the door.

She quickly backed away, her mind in a muddle, and headed to the captain's walk on the roof of their home.

So her father had hired an investigator and had kept it from her. Right now she needed time to think, fresh air and the calming influence of the Atlantic.

* * *

Noah Sheppard shook hands with Carl Daniels. "I'll keep you posted on any pertinent activity once I'm aboard the ship," Noah said.

"Sounds good."

"Noah, hold up a minute, will you? I'd like a word." Merrick said, as he saw Carl to the door. "Please enjoy the buffet table. I'll join you again shortly."

"Of course, Mr. Merrick."

Carl left and Merrick motioned Noah to a leather, tufted, winged-back chair near the fireplace. "Have a seat while I fix us a drink."

Merrick retrieved two crystal tumblers from the bar, then tossed an ice cube in each glass. "I don't know what would have happened if you hadn't done your due diligence…" Merrick shook his head. "I knew my company had problems, and that we were losing some business - the reason I sought this merger. But this…"

"You're close to bankruptcy, John."

"And a merger with you would solve that."

"I've helped turn shipping companies around before, but sabotage…that's something quite different. You have an enemy."

"I realize that. But the question is who and why," Merrick said.

"That's what I intend to find out. The merger has to benefit both parties. I can't jeopardize my family company."

"I understand that." Merrick pulled the crystal stopper from the decanter, then filled each glass with bourbon.

"With Carl's investigation into the matter," Noah added, "we should get more answers soon. In the meantime, I have my job to do. I'll talk to Farthing. It's important he step down as captain in order for me to have the respect of the men."

"I know."

"I'm happy to handle it," Noah said.

"Let me think how best to approach him. I'll let you know later tonight."

Noah nodded and watched Merrick fill each glass with liquid gold. "On the phone, you mentioned another merger, one of a different sort you wanted me to consider. What's that about?"

"Under the circumstances, I doubt you'd be interested."

"Tell me anyway." He shrugged.

Holding a tumbler in each hand, Merrick stepped toward him. "There's more than one way to merge two companies, or should I say, two families."

"Meaning what?"

"Marriage to my daughter."

Noah barked a laugh. But Merrick handed him the drink with a sober expression that told him this was no joke. Gripping the tumbler, he sat perfectly still. "You can't be serious." He shot a glance at the full-length portrait of a young woman hanging over Merrick's desk.

Merrick leveled him a look that spoke otherwise. "It's not the first time a merger between two corporations included a marriage. If both parties are in agreement, the result can be quite effective."

"That sounds rather cold-hearted."

"Not cold-hearted, practical."

"And just what does the lady in question think about your plan?"

"She'll hear nothing of it."

"Well, good for her."

"I realize this is the twenty-first century," Merrick said. "My grandparents had an arranged marriage, you know. My grandfather used to tell the story of when he lifted the veil on his bride, and how it was love at first sight."

"How romantic. The answer is no."

"Please. Hear me out."

Noah threw back his drink and stood. "Sorry. No can do. So, if you'll excuse me, I'll take my leave."

"Aren't you the least bit curious? My daughter—"

"Stop right there." He glanced at the painting. The woman's face was without emotion, blank even. "The portrait on the wall has told me all I need to know."

"On the contrary, don't let her stoic expression fool you," Merrick gazed at the painting. "The portrait only captures a particularly diffi-cult moment in time and barely scratches Miranda's surface. And even then it doesn't reveal how remarkable she is."

"Spoken like a loving father. But I'm afraid the answer is still no. I'm here to captain the *Elle Merrick* and to do my own investigation into the situation. And unless that's changed since I entered this room, the only merger I'm interested in is that of our two shipping lines. "No one comes close to your knowledge and understanding of the financial, mar-keting, and operational functions of our industry. Your leadership is bar-none. You took your father's insignificant company and in fifteen years expanded it to a worldwide shipping empire. And it's only out of respect for what you've accomplished that I'd like to help solve the mystery. You've lost your most profitable clients. Someone is out to destroy you and I'd like to know who and why. If it can happen to you, it can hap-pen to anyone in this industry. For all I know, I could be next.

"I've always admired you and your business acumen. But another word about selling off your offspring and even your business skills will come into question."

He set the empty glass on the antique side table and glanced at the oil painting over Merrick's credenza. The beautiful blonde dressed in shimmering silver, hair piled high on her head, stood stoic, regal, and unsmiling... And wearing far too much makeup for his tastes. It was hard to tell if she were full of her own self-importance or simply miser-able. Either way, he was not interested. He already had one nose-in-the-air female after him and that was enough.

CHAPTER TWO

Miranda stood on the roof of her home trying to make sense of what she'd heard downstairs. She inhaled the cold January air, but it would take more than that to untangle her jumbled thoughts. Placing her hands on the wood railing, she turned her gaze upward.

The North Star twinkled brightly, steady and fixed in the night sky. She thought about the thousands of mariners over the centuries who'd studied this very star just like she was doing right now. Charting a course in unknown waters, using it for guidance. Something she sorely needed.

She closed her eyes and let the scent of brine quiet her thoughts. She loved the smell of the ocean. For her, coming home was all about the fragrance of the sea, the memories it evoked and brought to the surface.

'Miranda you were born with salt in your veins.' A familiar ache squeezed her heart as she recalled her grandfather's words. He was the only person who truly understood her love for the ocean and the driving power it could have over body and soul - while her father would far rather stay onshore managing his empire. The seafaring gene had most certainly skipped a generation.

She gazed out over the dark waters of the Atlantic Ocean, the raging peak of waves barely visible in the half moonlight. She had to find out why her family's shipping line was on the verge of bankruptcy. A company doesn't just suddenly get there, especially with someone like her father at the helm.

John Merrick was a shrewd businessman. Forbes Magazine had called him the man with the Midas touch. How could this have happened?

She gazed upward, holding onto the moment as long as time would allow. With the party still going strong below, she reluctantly released the wooden railing and made her way back to the ladder.

As she descended the steps, she couldn't shake the image of the expression on her father's face - it still haunted. Her strong, dependable dad had stood, white-faced with worry and uncertainty. She gripped the ladder railing as an acute uneasiness washed over her.

She wasn't the type to stand by and do nothing. The future of the Merrick fleet, her future, depended on it. Tomorrow morning, she would board the *Elle Merrick* and seek her uncle's help and advice.

Jack Farthing was like a father to her. Having spent most of her summer vacations on board the ship, he'd taught her everything about life at sea, about what it meant to captain such a vessel. He'd know what to do.

She closed the ceiling hatch, gathered up her long skirt, then held onto the side railing and descended the narrow ladder that led to the top floor. She stepped onto the main staircase as the hum of chatter and merriment rose to meet her.

As she rejoined the festivities, she spotted Phillip Strong. If anyone could lighten her mood it was Phillip - a two-year veteran and youngest captain of the Merrick fleet. Dark-haired and sporting a five o'clock shadow fit for the latest cover of GQ Magazine, he was handsome, charming and rumored to be a scoundrel. His deep brown eyes held a twinkle as he took her hand.

"Phillip. My father told me you'd be here this evening. He'll be so happy to see you."

Phillip squeezed her fingers. "I hope you share his sentiments."

"Of course," she said. "How did you find our latest gem?"

"The *Sans Merrick* is a beautiful ship."

"I agree. Most people don't think of cargo ships as beautiful."

"We're not most people."

She nodded.

"So, how's it going with your father? Have you convinced him about sea school?"

"He'll hardly discuss it. I have more than enough hours at sea, but without sea school, he knows I can't captain my own ship."

"What about commanding something like Clayton Company's new super yacht?"

"I would so love that."

"You've seen it, then."

"Yes, but only briefly. This party has taken my every waking hour for the past two weeks."

"I can believe it." He glanced around the room. "Would it help if I put in a word for you?"

"Thank you, but he'll only see it as interference. You're young and—"

"Impeccably handsome."

She laughed. "That too."

"Let me know if you change your mind."

"I will. Enjoy the party."

As she left the generous dining hall, she spied her father in the foyer shaking hands with Carl, the man from the library. Their butler, Henry, assisted him with his overcoat, then he left.

She crossed the marble floors and approached her dad as Henry disappeared from the wide entry.

"I've been looking for you," she said. A knot formed in her stomach as she studied her father's stiff features.

He acknowledged her presence with a half-smile. His color had returned, but there was still that inkling of uncertainty and preoccupation in his eyes.

"I've been making the rounds to make certain I had a chance to speak to each of our guests," he said.

Not true.

He'd been closeted away with two strangers who seemed to know more about the family company than she did.

"Did you need something?" The brusqueness of his question surprised her.

"No, I just hadn't seen you for a while. Looks like you just saw someone out. Who was that?"

He glanced over his shoulder at the closed door. "A client."

"I know all of our clients. I didn't recognize him. Who's he with?"

Her father licked his lips. "He's the new rep for Eastland Freight. Come. We shouldn't be ignoring our guests."

You're a lousy liar, Dad. To lighten his mood she asked, "Okay, where is he?"

Her father gazed at her with a questioning frown.

"Your paragon of virtue. The man you want me to meet."

"He wasn't interested."

"What?" All humor fled. "But...he wasn't supposed to know anything about it."

Her father left her side, closing the subject. Odd, since he'd been so hell-bent on it earlier.

She hurried after him. "He wouldn't even meet me?" The slight shrill in her voice drew the attention of several bystanders. But her dad either didn't hear or chose to ignore her. Either way the whole thing was humiliating.

In her entire life, she'd never seen her father so preoccupied or distant. Always one to live in the moment, his tireless energy outshined even the youngest and fittest of men. But, it seemed her efforts to distract him with the mention of her *future prospective husband* hadn't coaxed him out of his misery.

Oh.

My.

Gosh.

She glanced around the ornate ballroom. What if the man were still here? Watching her? Could this evening get any worse? She sucked in a deep breath, raised her chin, and put on her 'hostess' face.

She wove her way in and around her houseguests - she was a Merrick, the heiress to one of the largest shipping conglomerates in the industry. Then she quickly suppressed all thoughts to the contrary as memory of that 'overheard' conversation settled in the back of her brain. She shook her internal head. *No.* Bankruptcy was not an option. She would personally see to that herself.

A second later, she caught her father's eye as he disappeared through the wide ballroom doors. The knot in her stomach tightened, and her heart ached for what he must be going through right now.

Bankruptcy, ruin, shame…

She would go to the ship at daybreak, before it set sail. Talk to her uncle and see what, if anything, he knew.

Chapter Three

Miranda entered the ballroom to a flurry of activity. A man lay prostrate on one of the sofas.

"Excuse me." She pushed her way through the group who'd gathered around him. It was her father.

"Dad." She leaned forward and took his hand. "Someone call an ambulance."

"No! Henry, my medication. Would you get it?"

"Yes, sir."

Medication?

Her father pulled himself to a half-sitting position. "Please, everyone, I'm fine. Go and enjoy yourselves. The night is still young."

"Could someone help me get him to the library?" she asked.

Phillip and another male guest assisted her and, five minutes later, her dad lay comfortably against the down cushions on the library sofa. Phillip and the other man left the room as Henry entered with the medication and a glass of water.

He took the pill, then laid back with a disgruntled sigh. "This will be all over the morning news."

Miranda started to speak, then glanced at Henry, who was hovering over her dad like a helicopter mom. He'd been with the family for less than a year. Because of that she found it difficult to speak freely regarding family issues in front of him. Her father must have sensed her hesitancy. He glanced at Henry and waved him from the room.

"He's all right, you know. Came highly recommended by Mrs. Nelson herself."

"Dad, what happened?"

He patted her hand. "Nothing for you to concern yourself with."

"Too late for that. Tell me."

He lifted a weary-eyed gaze. "It started several months ago. I had a complete check up to see if it was anything serious, but it was nothing more than a panic attack."

"Panic attack?" Her mind immediately went to the conversation she'd overheard. "What's going on, Dad? I went looking for you earlier and heard part of a conversation about our company."

He stared at her, then sighed. "I'm sorry."

"How bad is it?"

"Very, I'm afraid. I didn't want to tell you anything about it until I had more information."

"What can I do?"

"At this point, nothing. I don't want you worrying about this."

"Is that when the attacks started? When you first discovered there might be sabotage on our ships?"

"Yes. But so far it's only one ship. The *Elle Merrick*."

"Dad, you should have told me. What about…what about Captain Jack? One of the men in the room said Uncle Jack needed to retire. You're not seriously thinking about letting him go, are you?"

The expression on her dad's face landed somewhere between frustration and resignation.

"Don't tell me you think he's involved in this?"

"I know how much you love him and I do too, but at this point, everyone who has worked on board the past year is suspect. And if he's not involved, then relieving him of his command will protect him." He sat up.

"Here, let me help you—"

"No fussing, now. I'm okay."

"I'm going to do something about this."

He heaved a sigh. "There's nothing you can do. Besides, the *Elle* is in capable hands."

"I can't sit around and do nothing." She shot to her feet and stared at her portrait.

"What is it?' he said. "What are you thinking?"

"He saw the painting."

"Who?"

"My Mr. Right."

"Oh. You're not bothered about what I told you, are you?"

"I don't know. I mean… It's not every day a shipping magnate's heiress can't even *attract* a meeting."

"Don't forget beautiful."

Something between a groan and a chuckle escaped her lips.

"Yes…" John said. "He was here. He saw it."

"Well that explains it, then. Who would want to meet her?" She threw her hand toward the portrait.

"I love that painting of you. Even that ghastly bleached-blonde hair."

She rolled her eyes.

"As I recall, there was a time you loved it, too."

She folded her arms and continued to peruse the picture. "That's because I was twenty-three and full of my own self-importance."

"And all this time I thought it was because of that fortune-hunting fool you were engaged to – the one who turned you inward into a self-absorbed millennial after you discovered his only interest was your inheritance."

"Don't remind me." Her father's words cut deep. Shortly before that portrait had been painted she'd been in love with a man who, it turned out, was only after her money.

She'd been more than a fool during that time. Agreeing to a whirlwind engagement, believing his lies, and his vow of undying love, giving credence to the saying, 'young and in love'. Young and 'in stupid' was more like it.

Stripping the red from her hair and dying it blond had been nothing more than protective armor.

"After that hoopla in the papers, you simply wanted people to think of you as preoccupied and self-serving. When I know the very opposite is true," her father said.

She nodded. The media had hounded her every time she'd stepped outside the gates of their estate. Plaguing her for weeks after the break-up with news reports and articles filled with nothing but conjecture. The most painful was a series of articles called, Ship of Fools – playing off the fact she was shipping magnate, John Merrick's daughter.

The portrait artist had indeed captured her lack of joy and unhappiness during that time - the airs and false front she'd pasted on her face clearly evident in the painting.

She nodded. "That…and Mom." Her mother's long illness and painful death during that same time only added to the nightmare.

He patted her arm. "We were both affected by what happened to your mother. I wasn't the best of fathers then."

"Don't say that. You were and still are." She lowered to her haunches and placed her hand on his.

"I've often wondered if your desire to go to sea wasn't the result of that time in your life."

"No. That's the real me. Always has been."

"I realize that now. Wishful thinking on my part, I'm afraid. You've always loved the open sea."

"You know me so well."

"Thus my attempt at matchmaking."

"Which has obviously failed. But that doesn't mean you don't know me. It means you love me." She gently squeezed his hand and stood. "If you're all right, I should see to our guests. They'll be wondering about you."

"Good. Send Henry in. I need a drink."

She kissed his cheek. "I'll check on you later."

She found Henry standing vigil outside the library door.

"He's asking for you and his nightly bourbon."

Henry gave his usual, polite nod. She found his stuffy airs humorous, but endearing. She placed a hand on his arm. "Take care of him."

He briefly raised his eyes to meet hers. "You have my word, miss."

Such an odd, secretive, man, but her father trusted him and that was good enough for her. Besides, he came highly recommended by Mrs. Nelson.

CHAPTER FOUR

It seemed to Miranda that she had barely fallen asleep when her alarm chimed, signaling it was time to get up. The last guest had left at one a.m. She'd slept fitfully, waking up several times during the short night.

She'd had the forethought to prepare a backpack the night before – a toothbrush, paste, a change of clothes, including her passport. It wouldn't be the first time a visit with Captain Jack turned into a short excursion. If he gave the slightest hint she could join him, she'd jump at it like a trout on bait. Between the two of them it would be easy to keep tabs on her father with the satellite phone, and the Merrick helicopter could always be called upon to get her back home in an emergency.

Dressed in jeans, a heavy, dark hooded sweater and sneakers, she quietly entered her dad's room. He was still asleep. *Yacht Magazine* sat on the bow front chest just inside his door. She picked it up. The super yacht, *Endless Summer*, graced the cover. What she wouldn't give to captain such a vessel. She set the magazine aside and crossed the room to her father's bed.

His medication sat on his bedside table. Alprazolam. The name wasn't familiar and after a quick Google search on her phone she discovered it was, in fact, prescribed for the treatment of anxiety.

It was hard for her to believe her father suffered from panic attacks. A sure sign the stress over the company's recent losses had taken its toll.

If only he'd told her. She could have shared the burden, offered suggestions, helped somehow.

Her grandfather Merrick had started the line over fifty years ago with only one ship, The *Elle Merrick*. After her father inherited the company, he'd worked his entire life to build it into the multinational company it was today.

She could only imagine his fear of loss and the public humiliation that would follow.

She would not stand by and do nothing while someone plotted to destroy them. Could there actually be a saboteur?

Well, not on my watch and not without a fight.

She left a note on the bedside table with details of her plan.

Going to see Captain Jack. May be gone for a while. But will let you know. Please don't worry. I'll keep in touch. M

She'd board the ship, talk with her uncle, then touch base with her dad later in the day. If circumstances led her to stay on board, she'd catch a flight home at the next port. Her dad would most likely be angry with her for seeking Captain Jack's help, but if anyone could figure out what was going on, he could.

The grand house was quiet as she tiptoed down the wide staircase. She entered the kitchen, then popped a coffee pod into the Keurig and hit brew. While she waited for the container to fill, she opened the Uber app on her phone and ordered a car.

Seconds later, the distinct hazel-nutty aroma of the Southern Coffee Company filled her nostrils. She snapped on the lid to the paper cup, then slipped out the front door leaving the sleeping house behind her.

The North Charleston Terminal was just starting to wake up when she arrived. The subtle amber glow from the wharf lights fading as the sun rose in the east.

She thanked the driver and got out. A small flock of Seagulls peppered the docks like honeybees to their hive. A handful of stevedores dressed in their hard hats and reflective vests had already started loading containers to a cargo ship berthed next to the *Elle*.

Named for her grandmother, Ellen Merrick, the *Elle Merrick,* the smallest and oldest vessel in the line, loomed like a friendly giant before her. Miranda cast an admiring glance over her aging bow and stern. As far back as she could remember she'd spent the major part of her summers on board this very ship. As a result, the vessel was more than steel, it was her second home, and had become part of her very existence.

Her pride in the ship was due in part to her grandfather's accomplishment in building her when so much was against him at the time.

Growing up, she'd heard the story often. How he'd taken the last of his savings and his small inheritance and put it toward the construction of the *Elle Merrick.* At the time, he'd had a silent investment partner who had stolen her grandfather's design. Then got caught trying to sell it to a competing company.

The *Elle* had a heart and life of her own and Miranda was a part of that. She couldn't imagine what life would be like without her. The possibility of losing all of this was unthinkable. She made her way up the gangplank wondering if the damage to Merrick Shipping could be reversed at this point. She hoped Captain Jack would have some answers.

No one seemed to notice her as she neared the top of the ramp. A single deck hand strode by as she stepped on board. She took the stairs to deck 07 - the captain's quarters, then knocked. No one answered, so she turned the handle and peeked inside. "Captain Jack?" The room was empty. She glanced at her watch. Seven-thirty.

She left his quarters and made her way to the galley. Her uncle was most likely having a hearty breakfast about now.

The galley was empty except for the cook and one of the stewards. "Excuse me, but have you seen the captain this morning?"

"He went ashore, miss, right after breakfast," the cook said. "Are you a passenger? Anything I can help you with?"

"No, thank you. When do you expect him back?"

"I'm not sure. I'm afraid I'm not privy to that information." The man chuckled.

She forced a smile, left the cook to his duties and headed to the bridge. A young sandy-haired man stood at the helm checking the well-lit screens in front of him.

"Excuse me," she said.

The man turned, a note of surprise on his face. "Yes?"

"I'm sorry to disturb you, but do you know when the captain will be back?"

"He had some business in town and should be back around ten. I didn't realize we were taking on a passenger today. Welcome aboard."

"Oh, I'm not a passenger. I'm a…friend of the captain." She didn't know why, but she wasn't comfortable revealing their relationship. She found it odd not recognizing any of the crew. True, she hadn't spent much time on board since she'd graduated from college, but something about the situation made her uneasy.

The man raised a brow and the corner of his mouth lifted. "I see."

What the heck did that mean? What did he see?

"Captain's a sly one." He spoke low, as if to himself, but she heard every insinuating word. The man was her uncle for crying out loud. This whole thing was getting stranger and stranger.

"I'll wait for him on the main deck." She gave a curt nod and left. Once outside, she settled herself between one of the rows of containers near the bow. Her bulky sweater wasn't cutting it in the keep-warm department and the containers helped block the chilly morning breeze. Plus, it was the perfect spot in which to see her uncle's approach and stay hidden from view. No need to open herself up to more curious glances. She'd caused enough interest for one morning.

An uncomfortable sensation crept up her neck while she'd searched for the captain. Growing up spending summers on the *Elle* she'd known most of the crew members. They'd been like family welcoming her at the beginning of each summer break. Today, she'd been a stranger, gawked at by some and questioned by the others. Not so much in words, but in eyes that did not recognize her. It was sad, really. Almost as if she'd entered an alternate universe.

She shivered and glanced at her watch. Nine o'clock. Another hour until he was expected back. She vigorously rubbed her hands up and down her arms. What she needed was sunshine. The *Elle* was still equipped with open lifeboats - that worked for her. She headed to the nearest one, then lifted the canvas tarp and climbed inside. The thick, heavy fabric would act as insulator keeping her warm underneath.

Rubbing her hands together she hunkered down on the bottom and waited. Lulled by the warmth and lack of sleep the night before, she stretched out, slid a life vest beneath her head, and settled in for the next hour.

CHAPTER FIVE

Miranda woke to the hum of engines and the sound of water churning near the hull of the ship. For a second she lay quietly in the dark protection of the tarp overhead, the sun's rays wrapping her in a blanket of warmth. During her summers on the *Elle Merrick*, her favorite memory was waking up on her first morning at sea.

No!

No. No. No. She sucked in air, threw back the tarp, and peered over the side of the small boat.

Water. Miles and miles of water.

She glanced at her wristwatch. Three o'clock. How could she have been so stupid?

Her heart stopped. *Dad.* She dug deep into her bag for her phone. As she suspected… No bars. Even though she'd left a note with her plans, he'd worry until he heard from her. The sooner she called him on the satellite phone, the better.

She clamored over the side and hit the deck. Halfway to the bridge she heard footsteps coming from two different directions. Some protective instinct had her ducking through the nearest hatch.

The last time she'd seen her uncle was at her mother's funeral. To be escorted before him by some strange crew member was not how she wanted her reunion to go down. Ears perked, heart racing, she pressed her back against the inside wall.

The footsteps came to a stop.

"You must be the captain." The man's high-pitched voice sounded squeaky, as if he were nervous.

"And you must be our newest crew member." This man's deep, masculine tone held authority, but most importantly was *not* the voice of her uncle.

"Yes, sir. Pete Sanders."

"Welcome aboard, Pete and please call me Noah. We're on a first name basis here."

Noah? Her heart thudded.

"And no jokes," Noah said.

The crew member laughed. "Aye, aye, sir."

Miranda stayed put until the footsteps receded, then peeked around the opening toward the departing figure. Even with his back to her, she could tell he was a much younger man than her uncle. His dark, neatly trimmed hair and lithe physique was nothing like her uncle's short, stocky frame.

Who was this Noah person and why was he the captain of the *Elle*? And why hadn't she been told about the change? Her dad always kept her in the loop, especially when it came to the officers. More importantly, where was Captain Jack?

She exhaled a shaky breath, her mind in a whirl. Unless, he'd already been fired. But that was impossible. She found it hard to believe her father could have contacted him between the time of his library meeting and his attack. Someone else must have done it. That younger man had been set on getting rid of him. Could he have been responsible?

With a quick glance in both directions, she crept along the port side fully alert for any more crew members, then scrambled back underneath the lifeboat tarp just as one rounded the corner.

Hunger gnawed her mid-section, and she was thirsty. She'd wait a few minutes, then head to one of the guest cabins. It would be dark soon. Later tonight, she'd make her way to the galley – raid the refrigerator, then find a satellite phone. She just hoped she wouldn't freeze to death before then.

* * *

Noah entered the passageway that led to his cabin. Pete Sanders was young, and his nervous energy followed him with each step. It was hard to tell if the kid was anxious about the voyage or just overly friendly. He hoped the latter.

Friendly meant chatter. Chatter meant information. People responded to the likes of Pete Sanders - open, young, who liked to talk - Men with his energy were needed on long voyages and this crew would be no different than any other person who enjoyed lengthy conversations over dinner. A talker like Pete coupled with a good dose of whiskey made the quiet ones open up. Bourbon and cards were a sailor's friend. One slip of a word or a phrase is all it would take to identify the culprit.

If someone had told him that his quest to merge Clayton Company with a successful shipping conglomerate would lead him to this cloak and dagger stuff, he'd have said they were crazy. But what he lacked in skills, he made up for in instinct. He knew there was a rat on board, but finding him would be another matter.

He entered his stateroom, then opened the cabinet to his bar. He poured himself a drink, then sat at his desk and pulled a notebook from the side drawer. Flipping to a blank page, he entered Pete's name at the top.

He'd met each potential crewman during his initial interview, except for Pete. The young man seemed awkward and Noah wondered if their impromptu meeting had caused it. At the last minute, his first mate, Jim Hastings, had conducted the interview after Noah had been called to the Merrick estate on Saturday night.

Everyone on board, except Jim, had been part of Farthing's last crew, which meant one or more of them were the saboteurs.

After jotting down a few lines about Pete, he flipped back over the previous pages, scanning his notes on the other members. There was a page for each, except Jim, his longtime friend and first officer.

He perused each one, and had to admit nothing stood out about any of them. At least not yet. Gnawing the inside of his lip, he sat back in his chair. Neither he nor Jim could be everywhere at once, so this would take time, and fortunately for them, time was on their side. They weren't due to arrive in Sydney for three weeks.

CHAPTER SIX

Miranda used the glow from her cell phone to check the time. One hour since she'd ducked back under the tarp. Cold, tired, and cramped, she needed to keep moving. She slid from the confines of the lifeboat.

She knew the ship like her home in Charleston. Knew every crevice and hiding place on board. At least she had that going for her.

The dense rat-a-tat-creaking of steel against steel made it difficult when trying to listen for the crew, so a watchful eye was imperative. Any one of them could turn a corner at any time and spot her. A noise, a creak, however insignificant, caused her to tense and hold her breath.

Doing her best to stay out of sight, she crept along the deck until she reached another lifeboat. She climbed in and settled on the bottom. An hour later she checked the time. Nearly nine o'clock.

Most of the crew, except for the man on watch, would have retired to their cabins by now. Familiar with the schedule, she'd wait a few more minutes, then make her move before the next shift change.

Even though she'd rationed her water, she'd finished the last of the bottle over two hours ago. She swallowed in an effort to wet her parched throat, knowing full well the dryness stemmed more from anxiety than lack of fluids.

She lifted the tarp and peered out. Hunger pangs rumbled from deep within her stomach. First order of business, head to the galley while keeping in the shadows.

Glancing in both directions, she climbed over the side, planting her sneakers on the deck as quietly as a wharf rat.

The overhead lights spread a dull glow over the decks, putting her in semi-darkness. Even so, someone could easily spot her if she weren't careful. She moved quickly along the decking, slowing her pace when approaching another passageway.

She stepped right and made her way to the end of the passage, turned left and approached the galley. She peered through the opening and scanned the rectangular space. Under-counter lights threw a dull, yellowish glow onto the stainless steel equipment. Other than that, it was empty.

It took four strides to reach the refrigerator. She yanked open the door and began unloading bottles of water and plates of sliced beef and cheese onto the table. She twisted off the bottle cap and gulped half the contents. Her thirst quenched, she then slapped the meat and cheese between two slices of sourdough bread. She sighed as her teeth sank into the sandwich. The first bite was the most delicious, mouth-watering thing she'd ever experienced. As she ate she kept a watchful eye on the doorway.

Sheer nerves had her inhaling the sandwich. She quickly fixed another, wrapped it in wax paper, then stored it along with three bottles of water in her duffle. After a hasty clean-up job, she cracked open the galley door.

Coast clear, she continued quickly but quietly to one of the guest cabins. She knew from her earlier conversations they weren't taking on any passengers until later in the trip, so she'd take a chance and stay in one for the night.

On the upper level, she slipped her universal key from her backpack and unlocked the door to the owner's stateroom – her home away from home.

Using her iPhone, she panned light across the comfortably furnished room. Nothing had changed here. The same queen size bed, the oversized yellow rug, blue sofa and chairs with walnut side tables. A miniature refrigerator stood next to the built-in desk.

She continued scanning until the light fell on her trunk. The antique roll-top had belonged to her grandmother. The last time she'd had used it was four years ago when she was twenty-three, so any garments left inside should still fit.

Retrieving the key from her bag, she unlocked it, then lifted the curved oak lid. Except for a few clothing items and some personal things, it was pretty much empty.

Since it was late, she took a chance and turned on the metal bedside lamp, then shoved her backpack underneath the bed. She knelt in front of the trunk and rummaged through the garments – inside were two pairs of jeans, three shirts, two dresses – one long-sleeved and a sundress, and her yellow rain slicker.

As she reached for a small, framed photo of her as a child with her grandfather, she heard footsteps outside her cabin. She froze, staring at the doorknob. Only seconds passed, but it felt like an eternity. Still on her knees, she watched the handle turn.

Any second now… She glanced at the lamplight and groaned. Too late for that. Panic seized her, and she quickly threw one leg over the side of the trunk, then the other. Then crouched down and lowered the lid.

Something hard pressed against her right knee, and she bit her lip. She tried shifting her position, but it only made it worse.

The click from the door handle pierced the darkness. She held her breath as a heavy step thudded against the wood flooring, then another. A third step. Then silence - which meant he was now on the carpet.

The pitch black inside the trunk brought little comfort, as any second now she expected to be discovered. The silence continued, then several more heavy steps as if the watchman had left the room. But had he? What if it were a trick? What if he were still here?

Crouched in the fetal position, chin tucked to her chest, she waited —uncertain as to how much longer she'd be able to hold this position. At least the pressure on her knee had lessened. But any movement on her part would certainly give her location away. So she held as still as she could until light-headedness and the excruciating cramp in her left calf finally forced the situation.

Placing her palm against the rounded lid, she pushed. It flopped open, and she sucked in air. She unfolded herself and stood. The room was now in darkness. Her night visitor had turned off the lamp.

Relief flooded her entire body. Talk about a close call. He must have seen the light from under the door. She'd have to be much more careful.

Still wobbly, she limped toward the bed, knelt and then lifted a bottle of water from her pack. She took a long swig, threw back the bedcovers, and with sneakers still on, collapsed against the mattress.

* * *

At four a.m., Noah woke up fairly rested. He showered and dressed, then headed to the bridge to relieve Jim. He'd found it odd to see light coming from under the door of one of the guest rooms. Especially since they weren't taking on a passenger until Sydney. As such, there'd be no reason for anyone to have been in the cabin, much less leave a light on.

More importantly, he and Jim were the only two officers with passkeys and the only two on board who could access the cabins.

Why the shipping line had become a target was another question, but for now his job was to see that all onboard cargo made it safely to their specific destinations. The crew members were not familiar to him, but as previous investigations had determined, at least one person in this group was the saboteur.

That said, he'd called upon Jim Hastings to be his first officer. It was not only critical to have someone on board he could trust, but someone who could also help him. The idea was to catch the culprit in the act.

Even though the crew took turns on watch, he'd personally made his own rounds the past few nights, checking that all was secure. He'd not seen anything out of the ordinary, until this evening, when he'd spotted the light glowing from the stateroom. Coincidence? Maybe. But on the day of departure? Probably not.

Noah clipped up the ladder, then entered the bridge.

"All quiet, Jim?"

"It is. There's coffee."

"Thanks, I could use a cup." Noah stepped to the side counter and filled his mug. "I found a light on in one of the guest quarters?"

"Strange."

"Indeed." Noah took a sip of the hot liquid. "You still have your universal key on you?"

Jim pulled the key from his pants pocket, just as Noah pulled the second key from his.

Jim raised a brow. "So it begins."

"Seems so."

The men stood side by side in companionable silence, the constant chug-chug from the engine room the only sound.

"Elaina still coming aboard in Sydney?"

"Yes." Noah sighed just thinking about the extremely poor timing of her visit.

"No offense, buddy, but the last thing you need is Elaina Crawford compounding an already complicated situation."

"I know. It's my own fault for not cancelling her early on when this trip went from a simple, pre-merger excursion to one of undercover work to find a criminal. Once on board she will expect...no, demand... my attention."

"Have you even tried calling it off? She may hate you for it, but..." Jim shrugged.

"I made a few subtle attempts along those lines, but she didn't get it. So I had to be more direct."

"Like what?"

"Like flat out telling her it wasn't a good time to come."

"Are you kidding? You can't tell a woman like Elaina, *no*. It's catnip."

"And... I also told her I wasn't interested in anything more than friendship."

Jim threw back his head and laughed. "And she's still coming?"

"Yes. And no one is more surprised than I am." He shook his head. "I thought she'd understood. Instead I got an email that she'd be joining the ship in Sydney."

Noah took a swig of coffee. Elaina was gorgeous and pleasant company, but at this stage in his life he wanted more than a beautiful, manipulative companion at his side.

Most of his friends were already married with young children. He'd enjoyed his days as a bachelor, but he believed in marriage and was ready to fall in love, ready to share his dreams, and to grow old with someone. Elaina was just not that person.

"The sun will be up soon. Why don't you call it a night since my shift starts in twenty minutes, anyway," Noah said. "I'll take over the helm."

"Sure thing." Jim stepped aside. "Good night."

"G'Night."

Noah followed *watch* procedure and checked the GPS. He then recorded the time and the latitude and longitude on the physical chart near the helm.

This was his favorite part of the day. Nothing compared to the sky overhead…thick with stars. The ocean was a part of him. The smell of brine – the magnificent sea life.

There was a time he couldn't imagine being anywhere else but on the open sea. And if the merger with Merrick Shipping took place he would have the opportunity to stay ashore if he wanted and co-manage the business.

After he'd turned thirty, his years of a different girl in every port no longer held interest for him. And just when he thought he'd found that special someone, she'd left him for another man. A cruise ship captain, no less.

Jessica had claimed to love the sea, but after some time, he'd learned her interests leaned more toward the resort side of things. That had been over three years ago. Even though the breakup had been painful for him, love, marriage, and a family was still on his list. But, it was difficult to meet that special someone when always at sea.

In the meantime, he had a saboteur to catch. The merger couldn't happen until that mystery was solved.

As he sipped his coffee, he thought about his meeting with John Merrick and the man's proposition concerning his daughter. Merrick hadn't cracked a smile when he'd suggested it.

What kind of father tries to use his daughter for financial gain? Near bankruptcy or not, he could never contemplate such a move. At least the daughter had found it unacceptable. Or, had Merrick lied? He thought about the cool, aloof woman in the painting and Merrick's assurance that Noah's shallow opinion of her wasn't even close to scratching her surface.

As he gazed over the stacks of containers filling the deck of the ship, he wondered what it would be like to actually meet her in the flesh. She was certainly beautiful, if you liked the cool, unsmiling type.

Would she be cold and calculating? A user of men? It was certainly possible. Admittedly, her looks and her wealth could be quite an attractive package for some poor sap. Except now, even her wealth was in question, unless Merrick had put something aside for her in trust. Either way, no thank you, Mr. Merrick.

He'd never left a party as fast as he'd left that one. Merrick was nuts. His deal with him…simply, captain the ship, try to discover the enemy, and stop them before it was too late.

Noah had been all set to merge his shipping line with Merrick's until his due diligence uncovered some discrepancies. The fact that the company had lost business was not so much a problem, as he'd helped turn companies around before. But it was the how and why that concerned him. Could the answer be something in Merrick's past? If he could figure that out, he might be able to save Merrick Shipping and still find a way to make the merger work.

As for the ice princess – Could it be possible, with all of Merrick's fame and fortune, that in his arrogance he hadn't set aside anything for his daughter? Not even in trust?

Sure, he wanted nothing to do with the woman, but the thought of her losing everything she'd grown up with disturbed him. He'd also grown up with wealth and losing it all would certainly have its challenges.

He couldn't imagine the woman in the painting living anywhere, but there. To keep her in a life to which she was accustomed, was no reason to marry. But if he could save her family from financial ruin, save her inheritance - he would do it.

Chapter Seven

Randi sat up with a jerk. Fully awake, she checked her phone. Four o'clock. She fell back against the pillow, not even close to sleepy, after yesterday's untimely nap.

Minutes later she stood at the bathroom sink splashing water on her face. What she wouldn't give for a hot cup of coffee about now, but a sandwich and bottled water would have to suffice.

The sandwich turned out to be soggy so she tossed it, then sat on the edge of the bed. What now? Common sense told her she couldn't keep hiding out. Too many weeks at sea for that. At some point she'd have to reveal her presence, but when she did it would be on her own terms.

She knew the ship and there were only so many places one could hide. Then there was the issue with food and drink. Raiding the galley fridge might work for a few nights, but not long term. In the meantime, she'd hide out here. She knew the onboard routine, which helped.

She stepped over to the window and rested her head against the glass pane. Millions of stars twinkled overhead. Breathtaking. Her father believed the sight made him feel insignificant, but she chose to think God himself had created the scene just for her.

Maybe now would be a good time to roam the ship and most importantly, get her hands on a satellite phone.

She slowly turned the door handle, scanned the corridor in both directions, then stepped through the opening.

The galley might have a phone so she'd check there first. As she headed in that direction, her thoughts turned to her father. His chest pains had unnerved her, but at least they were caused by stress and nothing more serious.

The thought of losing him so soon after the death of her mother frightened her. It was imperative she reach him. The more time that went by, the worse it could be for him.

It was close to four-thirty when she entered the galley. She took a turn around the area, checking the counter and inside the cabinets, but no phone. There used to be three onboard, maybe more by now. She only needed to find one to make her call.

As she continued to search, she was starting to think all the phones had been locked up for some reason. The crew always had reasonably easy access to them during a voyage, but so far her efforts to find one had been unsuccessful. There had to be one on the bridge, but checking would be risky, as that's where the on-duty crewman would be. But, if she were lucky maybe he'd be on bathroom break.

She'd no sooner left the galley, when she heard footsteps approaching. She rounded a nearby corner and waited. The galley lights came on and she made her move, slipping past the opening without the crewman any the wiser.

As she neared the bridge, she paused. All seemed quiet except for the hum of the engines and the bellow of the sea underneath the ship. She stepped closer, then stopped at the first window, peeking above the metal frame. With a quick glance behind her, she crouched low and inched to the next box of windows until she reached the opening.

The bridge was empty. She realized the man on duty was now the one who'd entered the galley minutes ago. She'd have to act quickly. The risk of getting caught only lengthened as she hovered outside the entrance.

She stepped through the opening and scanned the area. A satellite phone lay on the top of the instrument panel. In three strides, she crossed the floor, grabbed it and dialed.

On the third ring, Henry picked up. *Thank God.*

"Henry. How's my father?" She croaked out in an urgent whisper.

"He's much better, but—"

"I need to speak to him."

"He's asleep. It's after midnight."

"Oh. Right. Of course." She'd been so intent on reaching her father she completely forgot the time difference. "I'm sorry if I woke you. How is he? Has he had any more attacks?"

"No, not since the gala."

"I left him a note before I left. Did he get it?"

"I believe so, but he's very concerned. With his recent attack, I'm not sure your absence is good for him."

"I know."

"Where are you?"

She had to make this quick. The man on watch could return any second, but some internal voice made her hesitate. Henry was still a relative newcomer and as such she was more comfortable keeping the facts to a minimum. The less he knew, the better. "Tell my father my excursion may take a bit longer than I'd thought. He'll understand from the note I left. Tell him I may be gone a week or more and that I'll call again soon."

"Yes, miss."

She hung up and quietly stepped through the doorway. She glanced left and froze. The crewman on watch stood a few yards away, completely still and in shadow.

"Hold it right there." The deep, masculine, voice commanded.

Blinking rapidly, she gulped air. The man stepped forward and she took off in the opposite direction. She flew down the steps - the thud of his feet-against-metal close behind.

Upon reaching the main level, she dashed across the deck, then ducked between a row of boxes and stopped. As her breaths ta-tooed against her ribs, she placed a hand to her chest to still her pounding heart.

Blackness surrounded her. She crouched low, focusing on the water churning near the hull of the ship.

It was impossible to know if the crewman was nearby. Between the roaring sea beneath her and the constant hum of the engines and machinery, she couldn't hear a thing.

She rested her head against the metal cargo box and wondered if he were the same man who'd come into her cabin the night before. Now that she'd been discovered, she couldn't very well go back there. That would be the first place they'd search.

If she could get her bag from the room, she might be able to evade capture a day or two longer.

She ran her hand along the metal side and stepped tentatively to the edge of the container. She had no idea if the coast was clear, but she couldn't stay here all night. She straightened and stepped forward. A powerful arm gripped her around the midsection and hauled her to a firm chest.

She yelped.

"Gotcha."

CHAPTER EIGHT

Noah was shocked at the feather-light person in his arms. His captive was too tall to be a child. But even a teenager on board would be a heck of a surprise. But as he caught his breath, he realized the small waist held tightly against his torso was all woman. He'd expected the saboteur to be on the ship, but a woman?

During his prep for this trip no one mentioned any stowaways from the previous voyages. Until now, the perpetrator had been a member of the crew. From the nature of the previous disturbances it was likely someone on board had been working with someone on shore. Could she be that person? If so, why come aboard now?

To distract? But that seemed unlikely. He had enough distractions keeping up with a crew he didn't know. But one thing was certain, the coconut fragrance wafting from the top of the red-headed, all-feminine form in his arms, was most definitely a distraction.

He released her waist but held tightly onto her left arm.

"Who are you? How did you get aboard?"

The light bulb overhead gave him a clear view of her face and slender body. Dressed in jeans, white sneakers and a dark hooded sweater, she stood, wide-eyed, chest heaving, lips parted. She was young, early to mid-twenties at most. The wind lifted and whipped several loose strands of red hair from her ponytail. She licked her lips and gulped - even though her face was free of make-up, her cheeks, most likely chapped from the cold, gave her skin a rosy hue.

If this young woman was a saboteur, then he was Captain Kidd.

She stood - sneakers rooted to the deck, staring up at him with the prettiest green eyes he'd ever seen – their shifting emerald lights holding him spellbound.

As he watched her, something flickered in their depths and he could see the struggle, the uncertainty in her expression - as if weighing what to do next. She opened her perfect mouth as if she were about to speak, but then thought better of it and clamped her lips together.

The spell broke. He blinked. "Have it your way." He didn't suffer fools lightly. No way was he going to let a…

Heart-stopping.

Vulnerable.

Anxious green-eyed, redheaded vision turn him into one, either.

Keeping his hand on her upper arm, he marched her below deck. As they made their way, he gave her a swift, sideways glance. She moved quickly, taking two steps for each one of his. Visibly panting now, the crease between her eyes held more annoyance than fear. She was a tough one. But so was he. Maybe a day or two in the brig would loosen her lips.

His second officer, Scotty, had just surfaced from the belly of the ship when Noah spotted him.

"We have a visitor. Caught her sneaking around the bridge." He glanced down at her. "She's not talking. Lock her up, will you."

Scotty gaped at her, then at the captain. "Noah, are you sure? I mean…"

"Fine. Get to the bridge. I'll do it."

Scotty gave a curt nod and left.

With his hand still on her upper arm, Noah led her to the lowest level of the ship. As they entered the compartment, the stowaway skidded to a halt.

"There's a brig?"

"She speaks."

Her eyes glazed over with apprehension and stared, unblinking, at the metal bars.

He unlocked the cell door, pulled it open, then stepped aside for her to enter.

"Since when does a cargo ship have a brig?"

"Since she occasionally sails through pirate-infested waters."

Wide-eyed and mouth gaping, she stood rooted to the spot. When she didn't move, he placed his hand to her back and gave a slight push.

The young woman dug in her heels, her back muscles tensing against the palm of his hand. She stood rigid, unblinking. Her earlier tough, annoyed manner had vanished, to be replaced by a troubled expression.

Intrigued, he watched her.

"I...I just need a second," she said.

What an odd thing to say. Her voice shook with a husky sweetness he found extremely appealing. For some inexplicable reason her resignation to her current predicament touched him.

Easy, Noah. She could be playing you.

He lowered his hand from her back and waited.

She swallowed, glanced at her feet and slowly stepped through the cell door, as if *willing* her sneakers to enter. She stopped inside the opening. For a second he didn't think she'd turn around, but in one slow robotic pivot, she faced him.

Her breathing had become quick and shallow, like a dog panting in the hot sun. In a matter of seconds she had it under control as if she'd done it many times before.

For a brief second her vivid green eyes held his gaze, before flickering over him - curious and assessing. What? Was she trying to intimidate him? He couldn't resist asking. "So. How do I measure up?"

"You don't."

Obviously, her recent discomfort hadn't lasted long. Probably figured her dramatic act was wasted on him. He was no one's fool. Better she learn it now, than later. "I'll get you some water and something to eat," he said. "I imagine you're hungry and thirsty."

She'd pulled her ponytail free of its clip causing her hair to tumble in a disheveled golden-red mass around her shoulders. Under the glaring indoor lights, the soft waves framed her ashen face. Her hands shook slightly as she pushed the strands away from her temples, proving she wasn't nearly as controlled as she'd tried to make him believe.

A dark substance streaked its black mark across her left cheek, highlighted by the stubborn tilt of her chin. Her intense gaze never left his face—

As if daring him to close the door.

As if he had no right.

After a long, extremely interesting stare-down, he slowly and deliberately placed his hand on the bars and pushed. It clicked shut, and she visibly jumped. So, she'd been locked-up before. She was awfully young to have already spent time in the pen. He pulled himself up short.

Not his problem.

* * *

Miranda stepped forward, gripped the bars and released her breath as she watched the captain's departing back. She glanced toward the ceiling and turned to face the cot as if that would ease the sudden onset of dry mouth and rising panic that swept over her flesh.

Her limbs quivered and she hugged her torso in an effort to stop the shakes. She'd always hated small spaces and this one felt painfully tiny.

She sat on the narrow bed, concentrated on her breathing and waited for him to return. Hopefully, with something other than a sandwich. These past two days were not how she'd imagined they would go. If only Captain Jack had been aboard.

Five minutes, ten, then fifteen and he still hadn't returned. Then she smelled it. The distinct, unmistakable, aroma of bacon.

Seconds later the captain, followed by a crewman, entered carrying a tray. She stood and stepped toward the cell door. The crewman turned his back to them and took his position outside the entrance.

While balancing the tray in one hand, the captain proceeded to unlock the cell. Seconds later, he stepped through the narrow opening and placed the tray on the cot.

"That wet rag is for your face."

She fingered the cloth, tossing him a questioning glance.

"You have a smudge on your cheek, right here." He lifted his finger to the left side of his face.

She placed the towel to her cheek.

"Your other left," he said.

She shot him an annoyed expression, then proceeded to wipe the other side of her face.

"I thought we'd have that chat now…while you eat breakfast."

"May I have my coffee first?" She laid the damp cloth aside. "I'd like to have a clear head if you don't mind."

"Not at all." He folded his arms and positioned his left shoulder against the cell bars.

Her mouth watered as she lifted the tray to her lap. She didn't say a word, just downed a strip of bacon, shoveling several mouthfuls of scrambled egg between her lips like someone who hadn't eaten in days, instead of hours. The coffee was wonderful and after several sips, she lifted her gaze to his.

"Who are you?" he asked.

Since she had no idea if he could be trusted, she wasn't about to tell him who she really was. She took another sip of coffee. "My name's… Randi."

"Randi what?"

She lowered her gaze. "Smith."

"Smith, huh?"

She nodded and shoved another piece of bacon between her lips.

"Miss Smith, I take it?"

"Yes."

"Okay, Miss Smith. What are you doing on board my ship?"

His ship? She twirled the fork between her fingers. "Running away."

"From whom?"

"My father." She swallowed. "He wants me to marry someone I don't love." She inwardly cringed. That was totally lame, but since it was somewhat true it had been the first thing to come to mind. Besides, she couldn't think of anything else to say. When he didn't respond, she lifted her head.

An incredulous expression had crossed his features. With her gaze still fixed on him, she sank her teeth into a piece of dry toast. It was obvious he didn't believe her. She chewed, picked up another slice and began buttering it.

From the corner of her eye she watched him shove his hands into his khaki pants. As she downed the rest of the eggs, she stole another glance in his direction.

"Finished?"

She wasn't, but his hands had already gripped each end of the tray. Before he could remove it, she snatched up the last piece of toast.

"Let me know when you're ready to talk." He strode from the cell.

"We are talking."

"When you're ready to tell me the truth, then." He slid the key into the lock and turned it.

She shot to her feet. "You're keeping me locked up?"

"You're a stowaway. What do you expect?"

"Come on. It's not like I could run away. Even cruise ships confine their passengers to their cabins when they…misbehave."

He paused in the act of turning the key, a humorous light in his eye. "Is that what you call it?"

She tamped down the temptation to retaliate with her own sarcastic remark, took two steps forward and gripped the cell bars. "I might even be able to help out."

"Really. How?"

"I'm not bad in the kitchen."

"I already have a cook."

"Look, Captain…"

"Sheppard."

"Sheppard, I—"

"What's your real name?" His intense stare unsettled her.

She wrapped her fingers around the bars. "I told you. It's Smith." Which was her grandmother's maiden name so technically she was one quarter Smith.

"Nope. Still lying." Tray in hand, he started to leave.

Blast it! "I'm claustrophobic," she yelled.

He stopped mid-stride and turned.

She licked her lips. She'd plead, grovel, anything to get out of this cell. "Please, let me out." She held her breath. A flicker crossed his tanned features. Compassion? She gulped and waited.

"Close your eyes and take slow, deep breaths. You'll adjust."

He continued toward the entrance.

"I came onboard looking for someone," she blurted out. "I didn't intend to stay. It was cold so I waited in one of the lifeboats for him to return. I fell asleep and when I woke up we had already left port. I swear. It's the truth."

The young crewman standing vigil outside the entrance turned to face Noah. "What she says is true. Several of us talked with her when she came onboard yesterday morning."

"Is that so? And who were you looking for?"

She glanced between the captain and the crewman. "The captain."

Noah lifted a brow. "Well, here I am."

"Except, you're the wrong one."

A suspicious gleam filled his honey-brown eyes. "Which captain were you looking for?"

She couldn't reveal her relationship to Captain Jack. Not yet. She searched her brain for another name. One of her family's other ship captains would work.

"Phillip Strong."

"I know him. He's on the *Sans Merrick*. Thousands of miles from here."

He still didn't believe her. Noah Sheppard was not a stupid man.

"Obviously," was all she could think to say.

"Why sneak around? Why not show yourself as soon as you realized your...mistake."

The sardonic gleam in his eyes had her lowering hers, but only briefly. Better to give him look for look. Be bold, Miranda. This man works for your father.

She shrugged. "I got scared, I guess. It was a stupid thing to do. The ocean can be quite frightening." She gripped the metal rods, pressing her face between them. "I came on board expecting to see someone I knew. Someone I trusted. Can you understand my fear when I realized I was out to sea with a bunch of strange men?"

The sardonic gleam in his eyes lessened, briefly softening as he studied her.

"Fine. I'll let you stay in one of the cabins…until I decide what to do with you. I'll put in a call for Strong later today. If what you say is true, he's probably worried about you."

"No."

"No?"

She gulped. "He…he… This is all his fault. It won't hurt him one little bit to worry about me. In fact, it might teach him a lesson."

He gnawed his inner lip and eyed her shrewdly. "Fine." He turned to the young crewman who had accompanied him earlier. "Pete, escort our *guest* to number four, then lock her in."

He started to leave then turned back toward her. "And the next time you want to hide in one of the cabins, you might try keeping the lights off." With that he left.

"Come with me, miss," Pete said.

Pete escorted her to the upper deck. As they passed cabin one, she said, "This is where I stayed last night. Do you mind if I get my backpack?"

Pete hesitated, glancing up and down the corridor. "Okay, but make it quick."

Once inside, she hit the floor and pulled the bag from under the bed. Pete stood outside the entrance with his back to her. Keeping her eye on him, she slipped her passport from the knapsack, stashed it inside the roll-top trunk, then locked it.

Two minutes later, she emerged with her pack clutched to her chest. They continued down the hallway to cabin four. Pete unlocked the door and stood aside for her to enter. She stepped through the opening, then turned to face him. "Hey, listen…thanks for what you said earlier, when the captain questioned me."

He shrugged and smiled shyly. "No problem."

She smiled back. It wouldn't hurt to have a friend on board. Pete, who appeared to be about her age, was pleasant looking with his head of dark curls and five o'clock shadow. She stuck out her hand. "I'm Randi."

"Pete Sanders," he said, his lopsided grin adding to his appeal.

"Well, I guess I'll see you when it's time for my next meal."

"I guess." He chuckled and, as he started to pull the door closed, the captain entered the hallway.

"Pete, you're needed in the galley. I'll take it from here."

Noah followed her into the cabin and relieved her of the backpack. Randi clenched her fists, tamping down the instinct to snatch it back. If he found the key, she'd be done for.

Without saying a word, he dumped the contents on the bed. She held her breath as he ran his hands over the meager contents.

He eyed the items, then turned his attention to her. "This is everything you brought on board?"

She pressed her lips together and nodded.

"No passport, driver's license, money or credit cards?"

She stuffed her hands into her pockets and shrugged. "I was…in a hurry."

"Right." He leveled her with a look that pretty much said she was a liar.

The captain strode from the room, turned, and shut the door.

She stood silently while he locked it from the outside. Heaving a sigh, she plopped down on the coverlet and slid the satchel beside her. She checked the hidden pocket. The key was still safely tucked in its hiding place. She pulled it out.

"Too bad, Captain." She twirled the key in front of her face. "I'll come and go as I like."

But for the time being, she'd co-operate, only using the key when absolutely necessary.

Chapter Nine

After a well-needed and nice long shower, Randi got dressed. She'd just stretched out on top of the bed, when someone knocked on the door.

"Yes. Come in." She crossed the room as the lock turned and clicked. Pete stood in the opening.

"The captain would like to see you in his quarters."

The captain's suite was a combination bedroom and sitting room with an office attached. There were two entrances to his office, one from the sitting room and one from the corridor. She was surprised when Pete knocked on the door to the suite instead of the one to the office.

"Thanks, Pete," Noah said.

Noah motioned to Randi to take a seat. She chose to sit on the brown leather sofa while he grabbed two mugs from a corner cabinet.

"Coffee?"

"Yes, thank you." While he poured the hot liquid she glanced around the room. It still looked every bit the captain's quarters with its wood paneling, brown leather chairs, and nautical charts. It was a room she knew well, having spent many wonderful evenings here, first with her grandfather and then later, with her uncle - playing cards and listening to their tales about life at sea.

"My first inclination was to have you put off the ship at the next port and let the local authorities deal with you," the captain said. "But after some reflection I decided to let you stay until we get back to Charleston."

"Why?"

"Whatever you may think of me, it's not my practice to leave a young American woman, law breaker or not, in a foreign country without a passport." He handed her a cup, then took the seat opposite. "I also reported you to Merrick Shipping and interestingly enough, they didn't seem too concerned about you." He flicked his gaze over her. "The head of security suggested I put you off at the nearest port. I told him that was unacceptable and he then assured me that Merrick Shipping would support whatever I decided."

She cleared her throat and glanced at the cup between her fingers.

"So, here's what's going to happen. You're going to work for room and board. Any missteps on your part, you'll find yourself back in the brig. You get one chance here. Please be aware, I will be watching you and if I have any reason to believe you are up to no good, or have lied to me about your situation, you will be arrested. Is that clear?"

"Yes."

"Good. You'll not be allowed to go anywhere on this ship except to work, then back to your cabin. Any possible future privileges will depend on how you handle that one."

To play the part she couldn't help but say, "If only Phillip had been captain instead of you. How different my life would be right now."

He shook his head.

"You disapprove?"

"I know Phillip Strong and frankly," he flicked his gaze over her, "you're not his type."

Randi tilted her head to the side. "You must know him quite well."

Noah's gaze locked onto hers. "We reach our next port three weeks from now."

"And where will that be?"

"Sydney, Australia."

"I see." She took a hasty sip, stinging her tongue in the process. She pressed her lips together and slapped her fingers to her mouth.

Noah grabbed a bottle of water from the small fridge. "Here, this should help."

He leveled her with a pensive expression.

"Thanks." The captain was a hard man to read. He perplexed and intrigued. One second threatening the brig and worse - the next offering ice for an insignificant burn.

He exuded self-control and his penetrating stare and disapproving features held her spellbound. Hard to imagine those firm, uncompromising lips curved into a smile. Did the man ever let down his guard?

He moved back to his chair, sat down and crossed his legs at the ankles. "You'll be responsible for cleaning all living quarters - mine, the crew's and the guest compartments when needed. We'll have a guest coming on board in Sydney, and I'll need you to make sure her quarters are cleaned and made ready for her arrival. I'm putting her in stateroom one. You should have no trouble finding it as I believe that's where you spent your first night."

She locked her gaze with his, licked her lips, then continued sipping her coffee, careful of her tongue.

"Any questions?"

"Yes." She clutched the mug to her chest. "Why do you dislike Captain Strong?"

A flash of surprise lit his eyes, then disappeared. "I have my reasons." He stood abruptly, putting an end to the discussion. "You can start work this afternoon, after lunch." He stepped over to the door and pulled it open. Pete, show Miss Smith where the cleaning supplies are."

"Yes, sir."

"Pete, you can drop the sir."

Pete nodded.

Randi set her coffee cup on the round side table and followed the young crewman out.

* * *

Noah poured another coffee, then sat at his desk to wait for Jim. Since the day Merrick brought him on as captain, he'd spent most of his days getting to know the crew. Each one of them had served under Farthing during the man's last three excursions and each one had still been eager to crew this vessel, even after Farthing's departure. Most importantly to Noah, all had been present and in key positions, from purser to chief engineer.

Jim arrived and took a seat across from Noah's desk.

"Coffee?"

"No thanks."

"According to Carl Daniels, for the past ten months, there'd been one incident after another," Noah said. "Nothing life threatening—"

"But enough to delay the delivery of millions of dollars' worth of goods."

"Exactly. But this last trip, engineering suffered mechanical failure shutting down the *Elle* for more than a day. By the time repairs were made, they'd missed dozens of delivery deadlines - costing billions in revenue."

"Sounds like the sabotage has gotten more serious," Jim said.

"And possibly more dangerous."

"From what you've already told me, until this prior trip, all previous disruptions could have easily been carried out by someone on shore before the *Elle* ever left port."

"That's right," Noah said. "Either way, we have reason to believe he's on the *Elle* now, which gives us the opportunity to catch him red-handed."

"How does Farthing fit into all this?"

"I interviewed him at length." Noah shrugged. "My gut tells me he's not involved – for whatever that's worth."

As soon as Jim left, Noah got up and refilled his mug. Back at his desk, he drummed his fingers along the wooden edge, deep in thought. This last disruption *could* have been carried out by one person, but seemed unlikely. He thought about Farthing. The aging gentleman seemed to be an all-around good guy, a fine captain and able seaman - and an asset to Merrick Shipping.

Afterward it was Jack who'd made the decision to step down for his safety. Between the two of them it had been decided to keep the crew to the minimum number of personnel necessary to safely navigate and operate the vessel. In this case, twelve, adding only Jim Hastings as first mate so Noah would have someone on board he knew he could trust. If anything happened out of the ordinary, he or Jim would know.

As he cradled the lukewarm mug in his hands, he thought about his most recent problem. His preparation for anything out of the ordinary on this voyage hadn't included her.

The auburn-haired, green-eyed woman was stunning, like a siren who lured unsuspecting sailors to shipwreck and death. Was that Randi Smith's purpose? To lure, entice, and distract?

It had been enough of a challenge to keep an eye on ten men. But without a doubt, her appearance had thrown a wrench in the works. If she were part of a possible ring, he'd need to keep her on board.

Threatening her removal from the ship had been Jim's idea. If she fought to stay, that could be a sign she might actually be involved.

He had no idea if she were here merely as a distraction or if she were an integral part of the saboteurs. If she were part of the plan to bring mishap to the ship, she might be the link to catching the criminals once and for all. Far be it from him to stand in her way.

Either way, he and Jim would watch her every move. He'd keep her confinement to one week, then give her more freedom, allowing them to track her comings and goings.

And if she turned out to be some foolish young woman who'd boarded the wrong ship in search for her lover, then she'd not pose any real trouble.

His stowaway's riveting, green gaze and her perfectly formed heart-shaped mouth filled his mind's eye.

Right. No trouble at all.

His handheld radio beeped, bringing him out of his musings.

He grabbed the device and pressed the down arrow. "Yes."

It was Eric, the chief engineer.

"Noah, we have a problem in the engine room."

"I'll be right there."

Noah stepped off the lift and strode across the metal decking. Eric stood near the electrical equipment holding an over-sized wrench of some sort.

"What happened?"

"I found a spanner wrench. Someone adjusted it to clip over this bolt." He lifted the heavy tool and pointed it toward the equipment panel. "If I hadn't seen it, the merest jolt would have sent it across the electric circuit below."

"Short-circuiting the power."

"Exactly." Eric blew out a breath.

"You're saying this was deliberate?" Noah asked.

"That's exactly what I'm saying."

Noah held Eric's gaze. He was good at reading people, but at this point the less said the better. "Okay. Keep a sharp eye out."

Eric gazed at him as if to say, *are you kidding?*

"Look," Eric said. "I've heard the rumors. Is this what I *think* it is?"

"And what do you think it is?"

"Attempt at sabotage."

"It's possible." Noah said, still not ready to confirm anything.

"I'd assumed the problems we had under Farthing were due to his age, but now," Eric stared pointedly at the wrench, "I'm not so sure."

"Has anyone else been down here other than those assigned?"

"Not that I've seen, but then," he shrugged, "I'm not always down here."

"All right." Noah nodded. "In the meantime, keep this to yourself."

"Of course."

Noah figured it was only a matter of time before this started to circulate amongst the crew. As he mounted the ladder to 02 deck, he hoped his instinct to trust Eric had been a good one. At least the chief had alerted him and not someone else. If the saboteur discovered the others on board knew of his existence, he'd be a lot harder to find. And Noah's hope that he'd eventually slip up would lessen.

One thing was certain - it couldn't have been the stowaway. She was locked up. But could she have been the diversion needed for the saboteur to enter the engine room undetected? And her onboard job simply to distract attention from the real issue?

He thought about her fiery hair and eyes the color of the summer leaves. Diversion or distraction. Didn't matter. Unfortunately for him, she was both.

CHAPTER TEN

Noah rushed through lunch, then stationed himself in his office to wait for Randi. He wanted a chance to observe her without anyone else around. Not yet ready to introduce her to his crew, he'd had lunch sent to her cabin with instructions for her to come to his quarters ready to work at 1:00.

While he waited, he contemplated how she might be connected to the saboteurs. Having a stowaway on board made no sense. But he wouldn't be worth his salt if he didn't consider every option when it came to her onboard presence, which in no way fit the culprit's previous mode of operation. Unless they'd decided to use a different tactic.

If, as he'd begun to suspect, they knew that Merrick Shipping was onto them, her presence could be a final attempt at destroying the shipping line.

Her tempting curves were most definitely distracting. And maybe that was the point. If that were the case, then someone knew a much younger captain would be in charge and what better diversion than a beautiful young woman under his nose for a month or more at sea.

A knock sounded, interrupting his thoughts.

"Come in."

Randi entered his office carrying a container of cleaning supplies and a mop. She stopped mid-stride when she spotted him. Her hesitation only lasted for a second.

"Reporting for duty, sir." She offered a lazy salute. "Where would you like for me to start?"

Cool and collected. It was an act, though, he was certain.

"The bedroom. When you're done there I'll get out of your way and you can work here."

She nodded and entered the sitting area and, as she passed his desk, he stood. "Hold up."

She stopped and turned toward him. She wore her hair as she had the night before – pulled back into a smooth ponytail. In the bright florescent light she looked like a teenager.

"How old are you?"

"Twenty-seven." She eyed him with a growing suspicion. "Why?"

He took the mop from her grasp, propped it against his desk, then took her hand. Fair skinned and neatly manicured, her fingers felt like silk. "These don't look or feel like they've seen much, if any, *real* work."

She yanked her hand from his. "And that's a problem because…?"

"Like any good captain, I'll be inspecting your efforts once it's done. If it doesn't pass muster, you'll clean it again."

"I'm sure you'd enjoy that. But I wouldn't hold your breath, if I were you."

"As a former Navy SEAL, I can hold my breath for quite a long time."

"Well good for you. This bucket is getting heavy, so if you don't mind, I'd like to get started."

"By all means."

He sat back down, knowing it was best to ignore a pair of sparkling eyes filled with suspicion. What could she possibly mistrust about him? Unless she was the saboteur – thwarted and disgruntled because she'd been discovered. That would account for her guarded expression.

The thud of the bucket followed by the obnoxious clang of what was inside hit the floor behind him. He turned to see her, knees on the floor, scrambling to retrieve the items. The words spewing from her mouth were hard to make out, but the frustration imbedded in her tone, he clearly understood.

He got up and, in several quick strides, stood over her. "With that mouth, you should fit right in with the rest of the crew." He bent down and helped her toss the last couple of items into the pail.

She raised her chin and glared at him. "If you must know, I was speaking French."

"A stowaway who speaks French. Interesting."

She shot to her feet and towered over him. He kept his gaze on her as he stood.

"But isn't it funny how swear words sound the same in any language?" he said.

Her mutinous expression reminded him of his young niece when she'd refused to honor her bedtime.

"I wasn't swearing...at least not in the way you were thinking."

"What other way is there?" He found himself warming toward his stowaway. If it weren't for the immediate problem with a likely saboteur, he might even find having her onboard a pleasant change. Deep strawberry hair – the mystery in her glances, which under normal circumstances would keep him up at night. Even with her freshly scrubbed appearance, Randi Smith was a beautiful woman. With a touch of make-up and the right clothes she'd be stunning.

"I've worked. On a ship just like this one. You know nothing about me."

"I wouldn't be too sure about that. First of all, I know you've run away from what I can only assume is a loving family, putting them through hell, and causing them unnecessary worry by your actions. Which, in my estimation, makes you an ungrateful brat."

Her chest heaved. "What makes you think I have a loving family?"

"Your obvious concern for your father when you were on the phone with him."

She shifted from one foot to the other. "And?"

"And...foolish enough to try and rendezvous with a captain who it turns out is on another ship. I find it hard to believe you'd make such a mistake. But you're even more foolish to throw yourself after a man like Phil Strong."

If she raised her chin any higher she'd fall backward.

"Think what you like, but that's not exactly how it happened." She glanced away and proceeded to squirt polish on his dresser. "Phillip is quite wonderful, and I'm sure this entire screw-up has been on my part alone."

"That's not what you said two days ago. As I recall it was something to the effect of, "Let him squirm.""

She snapped up a white cloth, then tackled the wood with frenzy.

"Listen. I know Phillip," he continued. "Trust me when I say he doesn't deserve some innocent's undying devotion."

Her hand stilled, her hesitation telling him he'd hit a nerve, as she turned her gaze toward him.

"Why, Captain, you sound like a man who's speaking from experience. Did you have someone's undying devotion or were you the one who gave it?"

He folded his arms. "My love life is not up for discussion."

Ignoring him, she continued, nodding. "You gave it and now you're not going to let anyone in, are you?"

"I suggest you worry about your own romantic troubles. In my opinion, any woman who runs after a man has her own issues to deal with. Life, love and relationships are far from simple."

She tilted her head. "Are you mocking *me* or true love?"

"Possibly, both."

"Maybe you just haven't found the real thing, yet."

"Or, maybe I believe what you call love is reserved for the foolish," he said.

"And you're no fool."

"You've got that right."

CHAPTER ELEVEN

Randi emerged from the shower feeling only somewhat refreshed after cleaning the captain's quarters and two other compact cabins belonging to the crew. Muscles ached in places where she didn't know she had muscles. She would certainly sleep well tonight.

She took her time drying off, patting on the last bit of body lotion she found in the bottom of her knapsack. She was about out of toothpaste, as well. She'd have to get more toiletries from the ship's store in the morning.

She glanced at her half-eaten dinner. She'd been too tired to finish and frankly longed for sleep. But it was only eight, too early for bed.

She slipped on a clean pair of jeans and a sky blue blouse, two of the items from her trunk. She'd just laced up her left sneaker when a knock sounded at her door. It was Pete.

"Here." He handed her a brown paper sack. "These are from the captain."

Randi opened the sack and peeked inside.

"He thought you might need a few things. It's a toothbrush and stuff."

"Thanks. I was heading to the ship's store in the morning."

"Well, this should tide you over 'til then."

Pete, with his fair skin, seemed out of place on a cargo ship. And he seemed so much younger than the rest of the crew.

"Where are you from, Pete?"

He glanced down and seemed to study his deck shoes. "Savannah, Georgia."

"I know Savannah. It's a beautiful city."

He nodded. "It is."

She'd hoped to get him to open up, but her question seemed to have had the opposite effect.

"Your first time as a crewman?"

"Second, actually." He let out an embarrassed chuckle. "Is my ineptness that obvious?"

"Not inept, just… a bit uncertain at times. You'll get the hang of it."

"Thanks. Well, um… I'll be back tomorrow at seven with your breakfast."

"I'm eating in my room, again?"

"Seems so, ma'am." He took her dinner tray, wished her a good-night and left.

Any guest on board a cargo ship ate with the crew, but she wasn't a guest. She dumped the contents of the bag onto her bed. It did indeed hold a toothbrush, toothpaste, a bar of soap, Old Spice deodorant stick, a pack of gum, a Hershey bar, and Motrin. She immediately popped two of the pain meds in her mouth and swallowed. The toothpaste looked used, but at least the other items were still in their packages.

She fell back on the pillow, crossed her hands under her head, and stared at the ceiling. What an unusual man. So, there was a soft side to the captain. Hard to tell with his assessing stares and probing glances… peeling back her layers like an onion.

This afternoon when she'd caught his eye, he'd stared at her as if he could see right through her. As if another layer had been removed. Except, he knew nothing about her. His opinion was based on false pretense. Totally her fault, but still… His earlier assessment of her actions stung. They weren't true of course, but it galled to think he thought so. He didn't trust her and why should he. She *was* lying, but had convinced herself it was for a good reason. Until she knew who she could trust, she'd keep lying.

The following morning at seven she was ready when Pete unlocked her door with breakfast.

"Captain says you're to deep clean cabins two and three before lunch."

She took the tray from his hands. "And afterward?"

"He didn't say."

"Okay, thanks."

Forty-five minutes later she entered cabin two. A slight musty odor hit her as she stepped into the room. The bedside tables and chest of drawers appeared worn and outdated.

The *Elle* had been the first ship in the Merrick line and the last one on the list to be overhauled. For the longest time she'd wondered why her father had put it off, but now realized it had to be due to lack of funds.

If their company was hurting financially, the beautification of this old ship would be last on the list for upgrades or worse, decommissioned and sunk as an artificial reef. The *Elle* was quite old and the open sea had definitely taken its toll on her. Any repairs at this point were probably too costly.

Randi pushed her melancholy feelings aside and made a mental note to polish the furniture. She cherished every inch of this ship and while the *Elle* was still seaworthy she'd care for her as best she could.

She glanced at her smooth hands and manicured nails. They had seen hard work and on this very ship. That smug captain had no idea, but the summers she'd spent on board she'd done her share. Any small part she'd had in maintaining the *Elle* had been a joy, and now that she was back it would continue to be. She stripped the sheets off the bed and got to work.

Seconds after she finished cabin three Pete arrived.

"Your lunch is ready."

She left the cleaning supplies and followed him to the galley. Fully expecting to see some activity, she was surprised to see the room empty.

"Where's the crew?"

"We've already eaten."

"Oh."

Pete nodded toward the work table. "Your meal is there. It's beef stew, French rolls and a salad."

She sat down, lifted the spoon, stopping mid-air. Disappointment filled her. She was anxious to meet the men and talk with them. It was imperative she find out who was sabotaging the ship. Without direct contact with the crew, her efforts would be hopeless.

"Not to your liking?" Noah stood at the entrance of the galley.

Her head snapped up. "Um, no. I'm sure it's fine." She dipped the spoon into the savory dish, then raised it to her mouth. It was very good and she was hungry.

He crossed the room and sat down opposite her. "After you eat, I want you to swab the port side of the main deck. Make sure you drink plenty of water and take several breaks. You'll need it."

As he stood, she paused, spoon halfway to her mouth and gaped at him.

"I left the mop and the other supplies in cabin three," she said.

"I'll have what you'll need waiting for you."

She licked her lips and nodded. Straight and to the point, he walked out without a backward glance.

Despite the fact that the man completely infuriated her, she couldn't take her eyes off his lean hips and broad shoulders. Since the night he'd snagged her around the waist, he'd taken her breath away. Any other time...

The deck seemed unusually massive now that she had to mop it. Normally, several crew members swabbed the decks together, each taking a different area. But today it was painfully obvious she'd be alone with the task.

Already tired from cleaning the staterooms, she squeezed her eyes shut and called to the surface any last remnants of physical stamina.

She marched over to the bucket, submerged the mop, then slung the soapy wet rope onto the deck. Swabbing right then left, she went through the motions, pushing the mop back and forth, before immersing it again.

A half hour later, ripples of pain shot through her lower back. She paused and pressed her palm to the area. It would take more than a short break to relieve the pain. She straightened up and inspected her right hand. Pinky-red whelps had started to take shape from the center of her palm to her knuckles, producing several large, painful blisters.

Squinting against the afternoon sun, she slid to her haunches and downed half a bottle of water. As she sipped the remainder of the luke-warm liquid, she studied the area she'd just finished.

She had the uncanny sensation that someone watched her and she lifted her gaze to the bridge. The captain stood, arms folded, looking down at her. She held his gaze, hoping like the devil he could read her thoughts.

If he meant to break her, she had news for him. There was nothing he could do to make it too tough for her. With her gaze still zeroed in his direction, she finished the bottle, then pushed her body up and off the deck. She grabbed the mop and grimaced.

The blisters were fully developed, making the task almost unbear-able. She searched for a rag, a piece of cloth, something to put between her flesh and the wooden handle. Finally settling for a wad of strands off the mop head, she wrapped them around her hand and continued with her labor.

It was another hour and a half when Pete relieved her.

"I'll take these." Pete glanced at her with kind eyes as he took the mop and bucket from her hands. "You can quit for the day. I'll bring you dinner at six."

"Sounds good. I'm starved." She offered a smile and received one in return. Pete was a nice guy and was only following orders. She could tell he hated seeing her work this hard.

He shot a quick glance at the bridge. "Think I'll call him Captain Bligh for what he's doing to you."

"And that would be a compliment."

Pete laughed. "I can see how you'd think so."

She pressed a hand against the soreness in her arm. "See you at six."

It was four-thirty when she got back to her room. She longed for a hot bath, but had to make do with a shower instead. Stripping off, she turned the water on full blast and as hot as she could stand it. She stepped in the stall, placed her hands against the tile, releasing a sigh as the hot spray pounded against her lower back.

She'd barely dried off when there was a knock on the door.

"One minute," she yelled.

Surely it wasn't already time for dinner. She slipped into her jeans and a clean shirt, then glanced at her watch. Five-fifteen. "Come on in." She sat on the edge of the bed, listening for the key. The locked clicked and the door opened to the captain.

As much as it physically pained her, she stood. "What, no dinner? Is the plan to *starve* me now?" She couldn't resist asking.

"I'm sure it would be no more than you'd deserve." He stepped inside. "I need you in the kitchen."

"Are you kidding? I'm exhausted." A rush of tears pooled in her eyes and she blinked them away.

"Our chief cook has fallen ill."

"Sure he has." She plopped down on the mattress and folded her arms. "If I had a nickel for every time I heard that one."

"Take these," he said, handing her two orange tablets and a bottle of water. "It'll help."

"Oh, I see what you're doing. Keep the stowaway pumped with pain meds so she can work day *and* night."

"Down the hatch." He folded his arms and waited.

"Fine." Any other time she'd be thrilled to be let out of her prison to do one of her favorite things. Cook. But all she wanted now was supper and her bed.

After she took the ibuprofen, she slipped on her sneakers and followed him out. As they walked side by side down the passageway she glanced at him.

"I'm surprised you felt the need to come get me," she said. "You could have sent any of the crew to do so."

"Maybe I like your company," he drawled.

Feeling guilty, more like.

"Or maybe you don't trust me with young Pete. He is rather hot. All that curly dark hair and all."

"He's too young for you."

She skidded to a halt. "I beg your pardon."

He grabbed her upper arm and propelled her forward. "No dallying. The crew will be expecting dinner in an hour."

"Well, lucky for you I like to cook."

"Oh, you won't be cooking." They paused at the galley door and he motioned toward the prep table with his hand. "You get to peel those."

CHAPTER TWELVE

Hundreds of potatoes were stacked on one end of the long stainless steel table. Randi gulped and stared. As the shock wore off she swung back to the captain. "You don't need all of these peeled. The crew will never eat all of this."

A red-haired portly figured man stepped in her line of vision.

"I'll leave her in your hands, Caffey. I'll be in the rec room."

Caffey nodded as the captain left.

"We peel for the week, Miss. Then, chop 'em up and freeze the rest."

That was not how they did things in the galley when her uncle was in charge.

"This is quite unnecessary," she said.

"Sorry, captain's orders."

"Fine." Teeth clenched, she sat down, picked up the paring knife and set to work. But the blisters in her right hand made holding the knife almost unbearable.

Ten minutes later she asked, "Don't we have a potato peeler?"

Caffey rummaged through a drawer. "Here it is, but no one uses it. I think it's dull."

"I could also use a pair of gloves."

"There's a glove for shucking oysters in the drawer over there." He pointed over his left shoulder.

"Perfect." Putting on the glove was painful, but once on, she took the peeler, placed it against the skin of the potato and pushed. It lodged into the flesh and stopped. She sighed and picked up the knife as Caffey placed a large bowl to the left of the pile.

"For tonight's meal," he said.

She nodded, glancing over her shoulder as he stepped back to the stove.

"With a name like Caffey and that red hair, you must be Irish."

"Through and through, as could be said of you," he nodded toward her matching head of hair.

"My great grandparents on my mother's side were from Ireland," she said.

Caffey lifted the lid from a sizeable pot, tossed in some salt and stirred. "The name's Sean McCaffey, by the way."

"Randi Smith." She tossed a skinned potato into the bowl, then picked up another one.

"I didn't realize the ship had two cooks on board."

"She doesn't. I'm only filling in until Cook is back on his feet."

"Well, something smells good so you must know what you're doing."

"Nope. Most of it had already been prepared when Cook got sick. Meat loaf, green beans, and I'm to whip the potatoes when you're done peeling."

"Nice."

"Yeah, for the crew. I'm no cook. I'm much better with machinery."

"So what is your job?"

"I help Eric with the engine."

"Second engineer."

"That's right. You know ships?"

"A little."

Thirty minutes later Randi set the knife aside and got up. She poured herself a glass of water, then stepped over to the stove. "I need a break from peeling. Can I help here?"

"Sure. Check the meat loaf. It has to be about done."

As she pulled open the oven door, a cloud of black smoke billowed into her face. Swatting the air, she took a hasty step back. "Um, I think it's long since been ready."

Caffey hustled to her side.

"Blast it." He grabbed an oven mitt spewing not-so-mild expletives under his breath.

Randi turned off the oven as Caffey set the pan on top of the stove. They stood, staring at the overcooked block of meat.

"I can't serve this."

"How long before dinner?"

"Thirty minutes."

"Is there any more ground beef?"

"In the fridge."

"If you'll slice enough potatoes for French fries, I'll take care of the rest."

Randi turned the griddle to three hundred and fifty degrees and got to work. Ten minutes later she had twenty patties frying on the grill. While the meat cooked she heated cooking oil in the deep fryer.

"Are those potatoes about ready?"

She'd no sooner asked the question when Caffey placed a large bowlful at her elbow.

"Ready to fry," he said, with a toothy grin.

Twenty minutes later when the crew entered the dining area, a stack of juicy hamburgers surrounded by all the fixings and mounds of French fries sat hot and waiting for the men.

"What happened to the meat loaf?" The captain asked as the men took their seats.

"I'm afraid I burnt it," Caffey said. "You can all thank Miss Randi here for dinner."

"It was actually team work." Randi met the captain's gaze, before turning away.

She enjoyed cooking and the crew seemed pleased with her efforts. If she made a good impression, maybe the captain would let her assist the cook the rest of the trip. After setting a second plate of sliced tomatoes on the table she stood in the corner ready to assist.

"Please sit down," Noah said. "We all eat together."

From her experience, she knew that was true, but was surprised he'd decided to include her. So far he hadn't, but since she was already here it might seem odd to the crew if she didn't eat with them.

But this was a good thing. It would give her the opportunity to get to know the men, make her own assessment as to their character, and to the identity of the saboteur.

"Thanks." She grabbed a clean plate and sat down in one of the empty chairs. The middle-aged, stocky man sitting to her left grinned. "I'm Eric Anderson, chief engineer."

"Nice to meet you. I'm—"

"Randi Smith."

"That's right."

"We all know who you are." He smiled in a fatherly manner as if encouraging her.

She glanced at Noah, who was eyeing her over the rim of his water glass. She lowered her gaze and reached for the platter of hamburger meat.

"Yes, for those of you who may not have already heard, Miss Smith is our resident stowaway," Noah said. "Seems she boarded the wrong ship in pursuit of her love."

A chorus of chuckles filled the dining room.

Completely embarrassed, she shrugged, her cheeks stinging with a rush of heat. Blast the man. Unfortunately, his deliberate attempt to humiliate her...worked. What she wouldn't give - right this very second - to reveal her true identity. See the shock on each of their faces, especially that of the smug captain. Instead, she'd have to be satisfied with counting the days until she could. She lifted the glass of water to her lips and drank.

"Well, at least I'm not afraid to pursue love," she said. "According to the captain that makes me a fool."

"Don't mind him," Jim said. "He's just jealous he hasn't found any-one yet." Jim grinned and glanced at Noah. "Isn't that right?"

The men laughed good-naturedly. Intrigued, Randi gazed at Noah.

"I'm sure Randi isn't the least interested in my love life or lack thereof."

"Don't let the captain fool you." Eric winked. "We hear he has a gal in every port."

The men laughed, again.

Noah shook his head while a smile played about his firm lips. He commenced eating, and turned his attention to the man sitting to his right, putting an end to the subject.

While he was occupied, Randi studied him. She found his dark hair, square jaw and deep honey-gaze hard to ignore. He gave the man next to him his full attention. Was it any wonder he commanded the respect of his crew and they, on the surface at least, gave it in return?

Her gaze roamed from person to person sitting around the table, ex-cept one or more of these men were saboteurs, out to destroy her family.

She let out a breath. Hard to imagine the captain could be in on the previous disruption to Merrick Shipping. Her short time in his company told her he was a decent man. Exasperating and totally mad-dening, but in her gut she believed him to be the real deal. And all 'by the book' when it came to her. Which told her a great deal about him. Even so, it was still too soon to trust him or anyone else on board.

Pete, who was sitting across from her, leaned forward. "Your boy-friend is one lucky guy."

Oh, gosh. "Thanks." Hoping to put a stopper in it, she raised the water glass to her mouth and kept it there. She drank until Pete's atten-tion went elsewhere, then set the glass down and turned to the man to her right.

"What do you do on the *Elle*?"

"The *Elle*, uh?" He chuckled.

"What?"

"It's nothing, really. But, only those who know a ship well tend to shorten the name."

Dang. He was right. She'd have to be more careful.

"So, what's your name?"

"Scotty McPherson. I'm a deck officer. I'm in charge of navigation watches and things like updating charts and routine radio checks."

She knew exactly what a deck officer did, but nodded, and gave him her full attention as if she were hearing it for the first time.

"We're entering the Panama Canal tonight," he said. "It's pretty cool, if you haven't seen it. It takes eight hours to go through the locks. It can get monotonous after the first hour, though."

"I've heard. But I'm pretty tired, so I'll probably pass."

Dinner went on in this vein for the next thirty minutes. Since mealtime also served as a social gathering for the crew it lasted an hour or longer some evenings.

About halfway through she started to clear the table, turning down Pete's offer to help. Once the plates and serving dishes were put away, she set out a bottle of Port and one of Bourbon with some clean tumblers and shot glasses.

With the last of the glasses in front of the men, she was curious to see Noah's reaction, if any. She glanced in his direction in time to catch the flicker of surprise in his eyes. Simply one of the many things this arrogant captain would soon learn.

At first she'd felt empowered by the captain's reaction, but a tiny voice of caution warned her to be careful.

Her years on board with her uncle taught her many things about life at sea. Day after day could lead to hours of boredom. He'd often told her, 'A hot meal, followed by a card game and good whiskey did wonders for the seafaring soul.'

Eric thanked her as she placed a shot glass at his place.

"I vote we keep the stowaway," he said, smiling.

"Hear, hear," several chimed in.

Randi felt a rush of happiness. This is what it would feel like to work at sea. Command a ship. Maybe someday… She glanced again at Noah. He'd already poured the Gentleman Jack and sat twirling the minute glass between his fingers, studying her with the gleam of a question in his eyes.

She snatched up the last of the dirty plates and left the dining area, wondering how many more layers he'd peeled away this time. Maybe she shouldn't reveal too much about her knowledge of ship life. He had enough reasons not to trust her as it was.

CHAPTER THIRTEEN

Two days later, while the crew was having lunch, Randi made her way to the captain's cabin. Using her universal key, she unlocked the door then crossed the room to his desk. She had to work quickly. Any minute now, he or one of the others could check on her in the galley. She flipped opened his laptop. Locked.

She rummaged through the top desk drawer, then the bottom. She was on the verge of giving up when she came across a thin, leather bound book. It appeared to be some sort of diary. With a quick glance at the door, she opened the journal.

It held notes about the crew, a page designated for each one by name. How odd. She glanced at the clock on the wall behind the desk - as tempting as it was to linger, she thought better of it and replaced the book. She'd been gone long enough. Better to come back later.

The galley was empty when she returned. She set aside several hot plates of food for the men still on duty, then cleaned up. Once everything was put away, she turned off the overhead lights and left.

She fully expected someone to be here to escort her back to her cabin. But when no one showed up she took advantage of her freedom and walked out on deck. She knew the dangers of going too far without someone knowing where she was, so she stayed close to the deckhouse.

The night sky was crisp and clear with a half-moon overhead. She inhaled deeply, reveling in the cool air as it filled her lungs. She leaned her arms along the railing and gazed out over the moonlit water.

Someday she'd captain her own vessel, maybe even the *Elle Merrick* or that gorgeous, luxury super yacht, the *Endless Summer*. She briefly closed her eyes and imagined herself wearing a crisp white uniform and deck epaulettes with four gold stripes and an anchor signifying her rank as captain.

Her thoughts traveled back to this evening. Dining with the crew had been the perfect way to meet them and learn their names. There was Pete – sweet, but such an awkward guy. She so hoped he wasn't developing a crush on her. Aside from that, it was hard to imagine him as the saboteur, but at this stage she wasn't ruling anyone out.

The chief engineer seemed a warm and friendly sort. His jovial disposition reminded her of Captain Jack. And Caffey—

"Beautiful, isn't it?"

Heart thudding, she whipped around to face the captain.

"Sorry if I scared you."

"No, just startled. I didn't realize anyone was about."

"Where you're concerned, Miss Smith… Someone will always be about."

She couldn't help but smile. "Why so formal, Captain? Since I'll be staying awhile, you can call me Randi."

"I'm simply following your lead, since you address me as captain."

"Noah, then." She rested her forearm on the railing. "I understand the ship is entering the canal tonight."

"A couple of hours from now." His gaze fell to her wrist. "What's wrong with your hand? I noticed you favoring it all through dinner."

"Blisters from mopping."

He gently took hold of her fingers and inspected her sore palm, the touch of his fingers sending unexpected shivers up her arm.

"Why didn't you use the work gloves?"

"What gloves?"

"The ones I instructed Pete to leave by the bucket. You didn't see them?"

"No." She shrugged and gently pulled her hand from his. "I guess I missed them."

"There's a first aid kit in your bathroom. Make sure you put some antiseptic on that before retiring."

"I will."

"Randi. Is that short for something else, or did your father want a boy?"

"You know, I never asked him. Speaking of my father, would you mind if I called him on the sat phone? I'm sure he's worried about me."

"Something you should have thought about before you snuck on board my vessel."

Infuriating man. She clenched her one good hand into a fist. "Is that a no?"

"Come with me."

She followed him to the bridge. With his broad shoulders and slim physique, he was certainly something to admire. Any other time she'd be terribly attracted to him, might even flirt a bit, but she pushed those thoughts away as she trailed after him.

The bridge had been like a second home to her during her late teens and early twenties. Day or night it gave one the best views of the ship and the ocean beyond.

"Here you go." Noah handed her the satellite phone.

She took the phone from his outstretched hand. "Thanks." She started to dial, but when he didn't leave she hesitated, waiting for him to speak, or go, or something.

He folded his arms and perched on the edge of the equipment panel. "Sorry, but I'm staying."

She licked her lips and gave a curt nod. Turning her back to him she finished punching in the number. She was pleasantly surprised when her father answered.

"Daddy. Hey." She stole a quick glance in Noah's direction and caught the sardonic lift of his brow. The man was difficult to ignore and seemed to relish making her feel awkward. He still sat perched on the edge of the panel observing her. She'd have to watch her words. Giving her identity away now would be a huge mistake. She cupped her hand over her mouth.

"How are you feeling?" she asked.

"Sweetheart, I'm having trouble hearing you?"

"I said… How are you feeling?"

"I'm fine. Where are you?"

"Didn't you get my note and my earlier phone message?"

"No."

What? This wasn't like Henry.

"Well, I'm taking a little…trip. It's a long story. I can't get into the details right now. But, I called to make sure you were all right."

"Where are you?"

"I'm on the *Elle Merrick*."

"Oh, that's good."

"Okaaay. Um…just know I'm safe and that I'm going to look into that *thing*…" She stepped as far away from Noah as she could and whispered into the mouthpiece. "…The thing we talked about the night before I left."

"Miranda, speak up honey. It must be a bad connection."

She squeezed her eyes shut in an effort to suppress her mounting frustration. She sighed and glanced behind her. Noah now stood, back to her, gazing out over the deck with his hands stuffed into his pockets.

"Remember what we talked about the night of our party?"

"Yes, yes of course. You're not doing anything foolish, are you?"

She glanced back at Noah. "Foolish is in the eye of the beholder, Dad. I have to go. I love you and I'll call again soon. Bye."

"Thanks." She handed Noah the phone, side-stepped him and headed out.

"I'll see you back to your cabin."

She didn't wait, just kept going. In two strides, he caught up with her. When they reached her room he placed his hand on her arm.

"In addition to cleaning cabins, how would you like to help out in the galley?"

Yes! This was the opening she'd waited for. *But, don't act too eager.* She pressed her lips together and glanced to the side. Gave it another second, then shrugged and faced him.

"You'd have more freedom," he said. "I would think you'd like that."

"What about Caffey?"

"Caffey's talents are better suited for non-food items."

"Okay. Sure. I'll help Cook out."

"You'd be doing more than helping him. Before I spotted you on deck, I'd just come from sickbay. Cook's malaria has flared up. He'll be out of commission for a while and may have to leave the ship. If he does I'll need you to take over for him."

"Of course. I'd like to help and I hope it isn't too serious."

"Let's hope not."

She stepped through the door and turned back to him. "And I can cook. The hamburgers were more out of necessity."

"Caffey told me."

"And I'm much better at cooking than cleaning."

"If you do a good job between now and our next stop, I'll give you the job. It'll save me from having to interview someone at the next port."

"I can do this."

"We'll see." They locked gazes.

Randi blinked and placed her hand along the doorjamb. "You know, as chief cook, I'll have to get up earlier than the rest of the crew. You don't have to lock me in."

"Nice try." He leaned in, grabbed the lever and pulled. She stared at the steel door and waited for the sound of the deadbolt.

Minutes later she checked the secret compartment for her key. She needed to finish her conversation with her father. The sooner the better. Now, where was it? She was certain she'd put it in the secret pocket in her bag, but it wasn't there. A bit panicked, she rummaged through the entire bag, then dumped the contents onto the bedspread.

She ran her hand over the items. It was gone. She searched the drawers and the compact closet. Satisfied there was nothing in the cabin that would identify her, she lay down and tried to relax. But sleep evaded her. The key was missing. Which meant someone had searched her room and gone through her things.

Chapter Fourteen

Noah took his time returning to his stateroom. Randi had now been on board four days and had yet to ask if she could leave. She'd actually jumped at the chance to stay when he'd told her she was needed in the galley.

Of course, he'd seen right through her feigned disinterest after he'd first suggested it. She may have thought her glib response had fooled him, but the light in her eyes told him she'd been delighted with the idea.

As he unlocked his room he wondered if he should be worried about mealtime. If she were in league with the saboteurs she could put something in the food to make them all sick. Maybe asking her to help in the galley wasn't such a bright idea after all.

Minutes after he entered his cabin, someone knocked at the door. It was Jim.

"You talked with her?"

"Yeah."

"What'd you find out?"

"She's agreed to take cook's place. Jumped at the chance as if she'd been waiting for the opening all along."

"Which might only mean she's tired of being confined to her quarters."

"I would hardly call being locked in her cabin at night, confined." He shrugged. "Maybe I'm just trying to keep her safe. Neither one of us know this crew very well."

"Not yet, anyway."

"But, I tell you what, her arrival can't have been a mere coincidence. Something else is going on here. I feel it in my gut."

"And you think giving her more freedom is the answer?"

"If she's the culprit, or in league with him, then yes. It'll give both of us the chance to observe her." Noah stepped over to the small fridge, took out a bottle of chilled water, and held it out to Jim.

"No thanks."

He unscrewed the top and took a swig. "That's it then. You're to keep an eye on her when I can't."

"You really think she could be the saboteur or working with him?"

"Hard to know at this point."

"I don't know, man." Jim said. "I mean…look at her."

"Don't be misled by a pretty face."

"She is that." Jim slapped Noah on the shoulder and left.

When Noah had taken the job, he hadn't reckoned on a stunning, green-eyed nuisance to occupy his days. She was the monkey wrench in the engine - the fly in the ointment - the unforeseen obstacle - the snag of all snags, which meant only one thing- sabotage.

Not necessarily *the* saboteur, but her very presence threatened to disrupt his well-laid plans to catch the culprit. And if she wasn't one of the bad guys, then she'd picked a heck of a time to sneak aboard this ship.

* * *

Randi jerked awake. Heart pounding, she glanced at the bedside clock. Five-thirty. She sank back into the mattress and closed her eyes. Last night she'd fallen asleep with the knowledge someone had searched her room. Rather creepy until she realized she'd been doing the same thing.

But why would someone search through her things? The captain would certainly have reason to, but so would the saboteur. Was it possible the intruder already knew who she was? She could stake her life on the fact that the captain didn't know, but not so the saboteur. At least the only document onboard to reveal her identity lay safely hidden in her grandmother's trunk.

Her mind clicked over every onboard crew member she'd met, thus far. Not one of them was familiar to her.

She thought about the media frenzy that resulted when she'd called off her wedding. It was possible someone on board could identify her from that period in her life, but she doubted it. She looked nothing like that heiress now. And until that time, she'd pretty much kept a low profile, only making the occasional appearance at some charity event.

Maybe she'd find something concrete when she searched the rest of the staterooms. But without her key that would be difficult. She'd only rummaged around two cabins already, the chief's and Pete's and found nothing incriminating – at least nothing obvious.

The quick glance at the captain's journal when she'd partially searched his suite was something. But until she could give it a closer look, meaningless. The fact that she had no idea what to even look for didn't help matters. She'd assumed she'd know it when she saw it. She certainly hoped so.

CHAPTER FIFTEEN

The warm Pacific was a delightful change from the frigid Atlantic Randi had left behind in Charleston. The balmy breezes hypnotized, and as pleasant as the weather was she couldn't let it threaten her mission.

She'd now been on board the *Elle* for almost two weeks and except for her missing passkey, there'd been no sign of anything even close to sabotage. Unless the captain knew something. Which was likely. And of course there'd be no reason for her to be informed. She was, after all, a lowly steward and a stowaway.

During that time, she'd spent her days rising early, preparing and cooking meals for the crew, cleaning cabins, swabbing decks, and had even painted a section of a guardrail on the port side of the ship. Exhausted, she fell into bed each night, then got up to repeat the routine all over again. She didn't mind, though. A cargo ship was a working vessel and everyone on board had a job to do.

She'd not had a chance to read any more of the captain's journal. Every time she'd cleaned his suite of rooms, he'd find some excuse to be there. She'd changed her routine, tried different times during the day, even during his watch, but he'd still show up - disrupting her efforts.

Until she realized he had to have been keeping tabs on her whereabouts as she moved in and around the ship. In a moment of temporary insanity, she'd wondered if she could distract the captain long enough with a bit of sabotaging of her own. Then nixed that idea as soon as it entered her head.

She'd just have to come up with another way to outmaneuver him. Then it hit her. She'd simply have to be more aware of *his* movements on the ship. As he was watching her, she'd be watching him.

Mid-afternoon, the day before they were to arrive in Sydney, Randi stood in the narrow library perusing the bookshelves. Unfortunately, there wasn't much here to interest her. She wondered if she should rectify that after she got home, but since most guests brought their own e-readers, there wouldn't be a need.

"If you have time to read, then I've not given you enough work to do."

Noah strolled into the library, pausing next to her.

"You do realize, maritime law says you can't *make* a stowaway work."

"That's true," he said. "But it also states, as captain, I can arrest you and keep you confined to your cabin, then put you off at the next port."

"Exactly. And that is why I *chose* to work." She folded her arms and gave him look-for-look. "Are you really going to begrudge me this one simple pleasure?"

He glanced at the poor selection of books. "If you can find something to read here, have at it."

The captain got a call on his radio. From his expression she could tell it was serious. And serious meant the good captain would be occupied for quite some time.

"Sorry," he said. "Seems I'm needed in the engine room."

This could be the opening she needed. His stateroom was down this corridor. On the way there, she stopped off at housekeeping, grabbed some fresh towels as cover, then headed to his quarters. Without the universal key she'd have to take her chances it would be unlocked.

It was.

Back at his desk she retrieved the book and continued searching through the pages, skimming one page after another, hoping to find something that would put the captain in the clear. She felt totally out of her league with the whole 'spying on the crew thing,' and having someone like Noah on her side would be a huge plus. She hoped he'd turn out to be one of the good guys.

She continued scanning his notes—

"Just what do you think you're doing?"

Randi popped her head up, and she slammed the book shut. She threw a glance at the office doorway.

Noah strode across the carpet and stood over her. Jaw clenched, his eyes glistened with anger. "If you're wondering why you didn't hear me - I came in through the bedroom entrance. Although as engrossed as you were, I doubt you'd have heard a bomb go off."

His gaze dropped to the journal in her grip, but he made no attempt to take it from her. "I asked you a question."

Her heart thudded against her ribs. Feeling very much like the kid whose hand got caught in the cookie jar, she shot to her feet. In her desperation she said the first thing that entered her head. "I brought you fresh towels."

"The bathroom is to the right, behind you."

"I know. I…I got distracted." She held out the book to him.

"When I said you could read a book, this was not the one I meant."

"Sorry. I didn't mean to pry."

"Right." He took the book from her hands and tapped the leather cover. "Find anything of interest here?"

Her eyes widened. "No."

"No? Then you didn't read very far." He tossed the journal on his desk, stepped around her and sat down.

"Everything okay in the engine room?" she asked.

He lifted his gaze, leaned back in his chair and folded his arms. "Careful, stowaway. Your persistent prying could get you in a mess of trouble - in more ways than you know."

She rubbed her nose, then quickly picked up the short stack of clean towels. After setting out the fresh ones, she gathered up the used, then walked back into his office.

She clutched the dirty towels to her chest like a protective shield. "That should hold you a couple of days." She glanced around the suite. "Anything else you'd like done, before I go?"

"Not a thing," he said, dismissing her.

* * *

The following afternoon, Randi heaved a large plastic bucket to the top of the ship's railing and dumped the biodegradable table scraps over the side. As a child, cook had given her the job of feeding the fish with table scraps from the galley. At the time she'd had no idea what biodegradable meant, but knew she was feeding sea life and that had been good enough for her.

Savoring the moment, she gazed at the ever-changing mood of the ocean. In the distance, a school of flying fish caught her eye. Overcome by a feeling of contentment, she headed back to the galley to prepare tonight's meal.

As she stepped through the doorway her right heel slid forward throwing her off balance. She sucked in air and clamped the bucket to her chest. Her feet slid out from under her. Right arm flailed, fingers splayed, she clawed through the air in hopes of finding something, anything, to break her fall.

The bucket went flying – she hit the floor. One second, two seconds, three. Chest heaving, she stared at the ceiling and sucked in a breath.

With a tentative movement she raised her head, then her shoulders until she'd pushed her upper body into a sitting position. She lifted her right hand to her face - her palm was covered in grease. Tilting her hip away from the floor, she inspected the seat of her pants - also covered in oil.

She'd spilled some earlier when frying the chicken, but was certain she'd cleaned it all up. Her first thought was she'd missed a spot. It had sloshed across the floor, but no way could it have reached as far as this.

She winced as she stood, then noticed the jug of cooking oil, cap off, near the stove. Someone else had been here, and recently.

She'd have to speak with the crew. There were rules. You spill it – you clean it up. Stowaway or not, you don't leave it for someone else to deal with. There were enough dangers on a ship without adding nonsense like this.

She limped over to the counter and lifted the near empty plastic jug and set it on the shelf behind the stove.

"What happened to you?"

Randi jumped and spun around. Scotty McPherson had stepped through the opening and stood staring at her.

"Careful." She pointed to the floor near his feet. "I slipped on cooking oil."

"Dang. You okay?"

"Yeah," she said, snatching up a dishtowel.

"Here, let me help."

She handed him the towel, then hobbled over to the closet and grabbed the mop and wash bucket.

"You…see anyone coming from the galley?" She watched his face for any inkling or sign he might have been behind this.

"Nope, but I've been on the bridge the past four hours. Wait…you think I did this?"

"Gosh, no. That's not what I meant. I spilled some after lunch. But I was in here ten minutes ago and the floor was clean."

"Then it's a mystery," he said. "Or a dirty trick."

"I guess."

Scotty strode across the floor to the coffee maker. "Just needed some caffeine."

"Thanks for your help."

"Anytime. Be careful." He called back over his shoulder as he left.

Randi took the stairs to her cabin to change. She stood in the bathroom, and twisted her back to the mirror to check for bruises. Then slipped on a clean pair of pants and a blue Merrick Shipping Line shirt. Now there were two mysteries. Her missing key and the cooking oil.

CHAPTER SIXTEEN

The distinctive white shells of Sydney's concert hall heralded their approach like welcoming banners as they cruised by Bennelong Point. The first time Randi had ever walked through their doors was on the arm of her grandfather. Eleven at the time, she'd felt like a princess that evening.

He'd flown her home the next day for her Junior Cotillion formal dinner and ball that was to be held at her home the following Saturday evening. She'd cried when he put her on the plane.

"Your mother is in charge and the event will be held at your house. How will it look if her daughter isn't in attendance?" He'd wiped her tears and cupped her face in his tanned and rugged hands. "It's part of your education. You are a young woman of means and someday you'll inherit everything your father and I have built."

That was the last time she'd seen her grandfather alive. He'd died on this very ship less than three weeks later from some sort of liver trouble. She'd been devastated and if not for her Uncle Jack, she'd probably have never gone to sea again. He had taken over where her grandfather left off.

She hung at the railing and continued to watch the opera house until it faded in the distance along with her memories.

Another week had passed without any more accidents, but the previous one still had her on edge. The more she thought about the location of the oil on the floor, the more she realized its placement had to have been deliberate.

Since the *Elle* emerged from the Panama Canal locks over two weeks ago, she'd grown accustomed to the ship's schedule and had developed a workable routine for herself.

During that time, she'd gotten to know the crew quite well, and had been dying to ask if any of them knew Captain Jack, but knew it would be dangerous to do so. So she did her work, engaging them in conversation when time would allow.

From her place on deck she glanced up at the bridge wishing like the devil she were the one bringing the *Elle* into port –signaling the tugboats with a blast of the whistle, docking her softly alongside the pier.

In the past, her uncle had praised her skilled hands at the helm. But, for now, she'd have to watch from a distance.

She turned her attention back to the wharf. It was a beautiful Australian summer afternoon. The sun shone brightly as the massive harbor cranes loomed like something from a Transformer movie as they picked up each megaton container off the docked ships with expert precision.

Even though she'd witnessed it many times over the years, Randi still held her breath as the crane lifted the container from the ship, plucking it off, seemingly with ease, before carrying it through the air onto the dock below. Flatbed trucks had already formed a line to receive their cargo.

She loved studying the brawny, suntanned stevedores working the docks, and once the *Elle* pulled into port the stevedores got to work. She wondered why they weren't using the most modern system to unload the boxes. The floating cranes would take some time, days even, depending on the delivery schedule.

Since she wasn't allowed to go ashore, she meandered along the side of the ship taking in the activity. She lingered there a few minutes longer, then made her way to the galley. The purser was to bring aboard more supplies and she wanted to make room in the pantry.

In the process of organizing the shelves, she noticed the cooking oil jug sitting toward the back. It was the one that had been spilled the previous week. Since shelf space was limited, she grabbed the container and unscrewed the cap.

As she poured the oil into the other jug, she spotted a small piece of paper stuck to the bottom. She pinched it off and was about to toss it when she noticed words written on one side. Curious, she set the jug aside and opened the note.

Leave the ship in Sydney or else.

Randi's arm hair stood on end. She stared at the note until the words began to blur. She blinked, swallowed, then glanced at the empty container. It must have gotten stuck underneath after the oil was poured out.

She shook her head. No way was she leaving.

Whoever you are. I have news for you. It'll take more than a bit of cooking oil and a threatening note to get me off my ship.

* * *

The following day, only four crew members, including herself, attended breakfast, as the rest of them were off-duty, spending their free time on shore during the two-day turnaround.

By the looks of things, all seemed to be right on schedule. If the saboteur were to tamper with the cargo, this would be the time during the off-loading. She now knew the saboteur was on board. The missing key, cooking oil and note attested to that fact.

Throughout the day she took her place by the railing as often as her duties would allow, strolling along the port side scanning the docks below. She'd witnessed this activity for many years and should be able to identify anything out of the ordinary.

While examining the pier, a prolonged squeak of metal drew her attention. It came from somewhere behind her. She cocked her head to the side and listened. There it was again.

As she neared the center of the ship she spotted the problem. One of the cargo doors had been left open. Odd. No one seemed to be around, either. It was highly unlikely whoever opened it forgot to close it, as the procedure regarding containers had been drilled into every cargo ship crew member since time began.

Seconds later she stood at the opening and peered inside. Hundreds of flat screen TVs, boxed and neatly stacked in rows, seemed to be in order.

She placed her right foot on the rim, grabbed hold of the door and hoisted herself inside. Except for the light at the opening, it was pretty dark.

"Hello." She squeezed her way between the single, center row. "Anybody in here?" Since no one answered and everything looked okay, she stepped along the metal floor back to the opening.

Still a bit uneasy, she jumped to the deck, making a mental note of the last four digits of the box number, just in case. This wouldn't be the first time a theft had occurred during the unloading.

In light of everything else going on, she wasn't going to take any chances this was an accident. She'd have to let the deck officer know what she'd discovered.

There were safety rules. No one opened the boxes during off-loading. She pushed the heavy door closed, slid the metal bar left, then down. Satisfied it was now secure, Randi curbed her mounting frustration and made her way to the laundry. She gathered the clean sheets into a basket, hoisted the linens to her hip, then headed out.

She unlocked Caffey's cabin, flicked on the lights and got to work. Once the bed was made and the dirty sheets in the basket, she tackled the bathroom.

The crew's quarters were much smaller than the officer's, consisting of only one chair, a single bed and side table with a tiny bathroom attached.

She entered the bathroom, and spotted what looked like a piece of cheese in the right corner. "Caffey, you're disgusting." Scrunching her nose, she tossed it then finished up the bath area.

As she turned to grab the bucket, a small sleek mass darted between her feet. She yelped and jumped into the shower stall. Randi's nerves crept over her like tiny insects. Heart pounding, she took a tentative step out and peered around the door into the bedroom. A rat sat hugging the corner behind the side chair.

She entered the room and leaned forward for a better view. "Don't think I can't see you." *Caffey, just you wait.* She huffed out a breath. "I guess that cheese was for you, little guy."

She straightened, pondering her next move. Supplies in hand, and keeping a sharp eye out for the rodent, she tentatively stepped left and he, thankfully, didn't move.

She was out the door in a flash.

She dropped off the dirty sheets, then headed for the stairs. On her way to the engine room, she passed the elevator and stopped. The thought of seven flights was enough to make her want to cry. The work she did on board was hard enough, but having to take hundreds of steps a day to accomplish all of it was physically exhausting.

She sucked it up and decided to take the elevator. It was undersized and she only hesitated for a second before entering. She pressed the E deck button and waited. She'd only gone down two floors when the lights flickered and the lift stopped.

"You've got to be kidding." She yanked the phone from the wall box and called the bridge.

"Scotty here."

"Scotty, it's Randi. I'm stuck in the elevator."

"Oh, man, that's not good. I'll send someone from maintenance. What level are you on?"

"Level 03. I'm on my way to the engine room."

"Okay. Hang tight."

She hung up and let out a shaky breath. Inhale – exhale. Breathe in – breathe out. She pinched a wad of shirt fabric, pulled it away from her chest and pumped it back and forth in an effort to cool off.

Why did she have to take the lift? She pressed her back against the metal cage, closed her eyes and waited.

Five minutes later she checked her watch - it felt like fifteen. Ten minutes later a sudden jerk, then the lift began to move.

Finally.

She pushed her body from the back wall and stepped forward. As soon as the door opened, she practically hurled herself onto the platform bridge. For a second she stood there overlooking the engine room. She gave herself a second to recover, then took the ladder to the lower level. The noise deafened, but she didn't care.

To her right a wiper stood painting the ship's bulkhead, while a young man, whom she assumed was an engineer, carried out the mundane, but necessary cleaning of the machinery.

She spotted Caffey next to Eric, heads together in what looked like a problem solving moment.

"Caffey," she yelled, more from anxiety than frustration over the rodent.

He turned and offered a cagey grin. "Randi. Hey. What brings you to the below?"

"If you're going to keep a rat in your cabin, then mister, you'll be cleaning it from here on out."

His face reddened, followed by a sheepish grin. "You saw him?"

"Yeah," she marched forward. "But, after it was too late. He scared the heck out of me."

Eric chuckled. "If you don't like rats, then you shouldn't be anywhere near this place."

He was right. Rats were notorious for hiding in and around the engine room.

"Well, at least I *know* they're here." She gave Caffey a meaningful glare. "But when I'm in a crewman's cabin, I don't expect to have one scamper between my feet."

"He did that, did he?" Caffey chuckled. "I suspect you scared him a lot more. But don't you worry, Randi. I'll give him a good talking to."

"You'll get rid of him if you expect me to do my job." She started to turn away, then paused. "So. What's his name?"

Caffey gawked at her.

"I know you named him, so out with it."

"Willard, of course."

"Oh right, after the boy from the movie who trained rats." She winked at Eric. "My pet rat's name was Wilfred."

"You had a pet rat?"

"I did."

"Wilfred, huh? Never heard of him."

"A scared, friendless, little rat whose only crime," she shrugged, "was being a rat."

Caffey gaped at her, his confusion etched all over his ruddy complexion.

"It's a middle grade book I used to love. But don't think that fact changes a thing. You keep the rat? You clean."

She turned and careened into the captain.

* * *

"What's all this talk of rats?" Noah raised a brow and glanced meaningfully at Caffey.

"Nothing, Noah. Randi and I have it handled."

Noah turned his attention to her. "So…are you planning to feed it for him?"

"Absolutely not. I told Caffey it was me or the rat."

"Good decision." He took hold of her arm. "Get rid of it, Caffey," he said, steering them back toward the ladder.

Once up top, Randi paused near the lift.

"I understand you got trapped," he said. "Are you okay?"

"Why wouldn't I be?"

"Your issue with tight spaces."

"As you can see, I survived."

"And yet I suspect you'd rather take the million steps back up."

She eyed the elevator. "You suspect rightly…"

"And yet you hesitate." Her pensive expression intrigued him.

She chewed her inner lip. "You know what they say, you get thrown off a horse…"

"Any other time I'd agree with you, but until we find out why it stopped no one gets on."

Was that relief flicking across her face?

"That works for me," she said, heading for the stairs.

They mounted the steps side-by-side. This was the first time he'd been this close to her since he'd held her around the waist the night he'd caught her on board. Close enough to notice the tiny gold flecks in her anxious emerald-green eyes.

She glanced at him. "What?"

"Uh, nothing. Just enjoying the view."

She blinked, swallowed and continued up the laborious flight. He focused ahead, holding back a smile. His compliment had been an honest one. Yet it had rattled - even flustered her. Another side to the mysterious Randi Smith.

They reached the main deck, and Randi excused herself. As she stepped through the inner doorway, he said, "I have a guest arriving in the morning. See that cabin one is ready for her."

"Sure thing."

He shoved his hands into his pockets, and watched her walk away. Her red ponytail swung appealingly back and forth as she pushed through the outer hatch.

Lately, he'd experienced an overwhelming desire to protect this young woman. Someone may have tried to harm her. The saboteur? If so, why? And what was the link between them?

Once inside the bridge, Noah called the engine room.

"Eric, here."

"It's Noah. I don't know if you've heard, but Randi got trapped in the elevator about twenty minutes ago."

"I know, maintenance just informed me."

"See if there's any history of past problems. I want to know what caused it. And no one uses it until we know it's safe."

"You got it."

Chapter Seventeen

The following day, only a handful of crew members attended breakfast as the other half of the crew were off-duty and already on shore. The saboteur had yet to make his move, so today was his final chance before they set sail in the morning.

With the last of the dishes done, she grabbed the sat phone from the counter and dialed her home. It would be dinnertime there and hopefully her dad was available.

"Hello, Henry. It's Miranda. May I speak to my father?"

"He's gone out for dinner."

"Oh, okay, I'll try his cell."

"His cell is here. You know how he is about taking it with him."

Actually, she'd never known him not to take it when he left the house. Disappointment filled her. She needed to hear his voice. Make sure he was all right.

"Let him know I called, and that all is well."

"I will, Miss Miranda."

Randi hung up slightly encouraged. At least her father was able to enjoy an evening out.

She took a break and positioned herself at the railing. The expert handling of the colossal equipment still astonished. The stevedores in their hard hats and heavy boots were well on their way to unloading the last of the cargo.

She tilted her head back and gazed at the container overhead. No matter how many times she'd witnessed it, she marveled at the engineering feat of the colossal cranes at work. Cables, pulleys and masses of metal and countless other moving parts she knew nothing about.

A sudden commotion on the ground caught her attention. Several dockworkers yelled and pointed to the box overhead. In that second, the container door flew open, sending hundreds of flat screen TVs through the air. Stevedores dove for cover while others crouched waiting for the inevitable.

Glass, metal and plastic lay splintered and in pieces on the wharf's surface narrowly missing Jim. She watched, horrified, as Noah and several stevedores ran to assist him.

It had to have been the one she'd found unlocked. She needed to check to be sure, but had no doubt the saboteur had been behind it.

The uncanny feeling she was being watched made her skin crawl. She spun around, and in an adrenaline rush, ran to the spot where she'd secured the container. But when she got there, it and the surrounding containers were gone.

This was no accident. Whoever opened it knew the schedule. She ran to the end of the row, searched right and then left. But her efforts were fruitless. By now the man had disappeared and could be anywhere at this point.

Dock workers had come and gone during the unloading. The saboteur could have been any one of them.

Back at the railing she watched Noah and Jim talk to the port authorities. A few minutes later, Noah made his way back up the gangplank. Stone-faced, he strode right by her. She hesitated, then hustled after him.

"Noah."

He stopped and turned. His anger was clearly evident now that she was face-to-face with him.

"Yes. What is it?" Jaw clenched, he stared at her with mounting impatience.

She licked her lips and swallowed. "What happened?"

"Someone tampered with the latch on that container." He folded his arms and leveled his penetrating gaze at her. "I don't suppose you'd know anything about it."

"I…yes…actually, I do."

"What do you mean?"

"Shortly after we docked I was on deck watching the stevedores when I heard the sound of metal hitting metal. I went to investigate and found the door open on one of the containers. It was filled with flat screen TVs."

"Why didn't you say something?"

She lifted her shoulder. "I closed it, and chalked it up to a curious dockworker." Which wasn't completely true. She had her own suspicions, but wasn't ready to reveal them. More importantly, she needed to keep her identity secret for as long as possible.

"You're absolutely certain you shut it properly?"

"Yes."

He ran his hand through his short crop of hair. "And you didn't see anyone?"

"I didn't." She licked her lips. "You think this is more than a curious stevedore?"

He nodded and seemed distracted.

"Why aren't we using the automatic stacking cranes to unload?" she asked.

"Traffic is heavy today and it's reserved for the larger vessels."

"Well it's not as safe."

"I believe that was the point."

Randi felt certain Noah couldn't be connected to any sabotage. Noah's reaction to this accident bore evidence to that fact. Maybe it was time she trusted him…just a little. Yet it was still too soon to reveal her true identity. Once discovered he'd most likely send her home and that would never do.

This was no game and it was painfully clear she was out of her element. In hindsight, to board the *Elle* like she had may not have been the smartest thing she'd ever done.

* * *

Noah entered his office just as Eric called from the engine room.

"Thought you'd like an update on the lift," he said.

"What'd you find?"

"I checked the line and voltage levels and the contact resistance of the relays. Everything seems to be in good shape."

"But…"

"I need to dig deeper. It looks like a short voltage dip may have locked up the system."

"Okay. Keep working on it. No one uses the lift again until it's fixed."

"Got it."

* * *

Randi spent the rest of the morning preparing lunch for the crew. Once done, she set the table with baked chicken, green peas, rice pilaf and hot rolls. The on-duty men had worked all morning on and off the ship and they deserved a hearty meal. The fact that it would take longer for them to eat than if she'd served sandwiches and coffee was also a plus.

She hadn't had a chance to fully explore any of the crew's quarters since her key was taken. Her cleaning schedule was so tightly managed by the captain, the few minutes she had between jobs simply was not enough time for a thorough search of each cabin.

Her plan was to sneak away while the men ate. And with half the crew still on shore there would be less chance of discovery.

The crew entered the dining area discussing the morning's events, especially the container accident. A few minutes later, Noah came in with Jim. They talked quietly and took their seats at the far end of the table. She'd wondered if Jim were the culprit, but scrapped the idea, now that he'd had such a close call.

He and Noah seemed oblivious to the rest of the officers who chatted heartily while passing the platters around the table. Whatever they were discussing certainly held their attention. Maybe this would be a good time to slip away.

Satisfied the men had everything they needed, she headed for the door.

"Aren't you going to join us?" Pete asked.

"I ate earlier. I have to get a stateroom ready for the captain's guest. She's coming onboard in the morning."

She hurried away before Pete got any more ideas. The guest rooms were down the hallway from the officers' cabins. She'd prepare cabin one after she checked out Scotty's quarters. She'd started cleaning it two days ago, but he'd shown up minutes later nixing any chance for a search. With the men in the dining hall, this would be a good time to continue. She tried the knob. Locked.

"Don't you need this?"

Randi spun around. Noah stood a few feet behind her with a key.

"Jumpy, aren't we?"

She snatched the key from his outstretched hand. "Are you following me?"

"You have a problem with that?"

"I do if your intent is to frighten me."

"I heard you tell Pete you were off to prepare cabin one. I assumed you needed the key. I tried to get your attention before you left but you seemed quite focused on leaving. He's quite smitten with you, by the way."

"I've noticed and believe me, I've done my best to discourage him."

He eyed the door in front of them, ending the subject of Pete. "This is not a guest room. And I'm certain you're not lost."

"Scotty came in while I was cleaning the other day, so I left it for later. I thought I'd finish the job, that's all."

"Efficient thing, aren't you?"

"I try to be, yes."

"You seem to be missing your bucket of supplies."

She squeezed her eyes shut. The man was absolutely infuriating. "I was going to take a quick look inside first to see what I'd need, if anything."

"Mind if I join you?"

"Of course not."

She unlocked the door and stepped across the threshold, with Noah close behind. Randi glanced around the compact space moving slowly as if inspecting her surroundings.

She entered the bathroom and glanced behind her. Noah stood a few feet back, watching her. Heat rose up her neck as she removed the used towels, then made a point of wiping out the sink.

When she turned to face him, the wicked gleam in his eyes told her she hadn't fooled him one bit. She raised her chin. "I think this will do for now. I'll bring Scotty more clean towels after I take care of cabin one."

"You do that."

She followed him out, then locked the door and faced him.

"Anything else? Or would you also like to take a stroll through stateroom one?"

"I don't think that'll be necessary. Don't let me keep you from your work."

Noah held her gaze. It was clear he didn't trust her. And just when she was about to start trusting him, too.

"Don't let your chicken get cold," was all she could think to say.

"That's the least of my worries."

Randi watched him stride down the passageway, wondering if there had been a double meaning in Noah's words. For trust to work it had to go both ways. Maybe if she gave him a reason to trust her...

Sorely tempted to go back in Scotty's room, she thought better of it. It would be so like Noah to still be keeping tabs on her. Instead, she made her way to the storage closet for the cleaning supplies.

Stateroom one was always reserved for the owner while on board. Under normal circumstances, that's exactly where she'd be staying.

The suite was locked when she got there. After she opened it, she slid the key in her jeans pocket, then set to work. The roomy suite only took about forty minutes to clean.

Once the bed was made, she plopped down on the mattress. She loved this place. It certainly wasn't the Ritz, nor was it the caliber of her suite of rooms back home in Charleston. But, it was colorful and comfortable and held the most amazing memories from her childhood.

She gazed around the space. All it needed now was flowers. When her grandfather was alive, he'd always made certain her room had fresh flowers when she came aboard. But, unless she could con someone to go ashore and buy them, this would have to do.

She spruced up the bath with fresh linens, then unlocked the trunk and retrieved her passport. Even though the trunk padlock was secure, she felt uncomfortable leaving it there. One simple request from a guest and the trunk could easily be opened.

About to leave, her gaze fell on the large painting hanging over the chest. She crossed the bedroom, removed it, then turned it over. It was still there - the paper tear in the back of the painting.

Reaching in with her fingers, she carefully pulled out her diary. It had been the perfect hiding place for the book that held all of her girlhood secrets.

She set it aside, then tucked her passport into its place. After securing the painting back to the wall, she gathered up her supplies and left.

Back in her cabin, she quickly shoved the trunk key underneath the mattress along with her pink and white diary.

She'd been gone longer than she'd intended and the sooner she cleaned the galley from lunch the better. Hopefully she'd have a few minutes this afternoon to search Scotty's room.

CHAPTER EIGHTEEN

The third morning in port, Noah rushed through breakfast. Twenty containers were being off-loaded, and he wanted to check their progress. And God help him - Elaina would be arriving, as well.

Minutes later he stood at the rail and watched the last of the containers leave the ship. The meticulous planning had been done and aside from yesterday's accident, all was on schedule.

Most voyages were pleasant, but the pressure to stay on high alert was taking a toll. The constant worry that something could go wrong was beginning to wear on him. Jim felt the same and had suggested they get someone on board to help watch the crew. At the time he'd nixed the idea, but now wondered if he should have. Another set of eyes would have been welcome about now.

As he lingered, Scotty strolled up the ramp holding a bouquet of fresh flowers. Noah blinked and stared, then turned to follow Scotty's line of vision. Randi stood at the top of the gangplank wreathed in smiles. Stunned, he watched Scotty place the flowers in her outstretched hands.

He had no idea what she was saying, but it was evident from her animated features he'd pleased her.

Scotty and Randi. Seriously? How had he missed that? He'd always thought of himself as observant, but even he had never seen this coming.

Randi accepted the bouquet, said something, then left. Scotty grinned, shook his head and made his way back down the ramp to the dock.

* * *

Randi set the vase and flowers on the refreshment table she'd prepared for Noah's guest then hurried from the reception room. Curious as to Noah's taste in women, she had no intention of missing the arrival of the captain's guest.

Stationed at the railing, Randi gazed out over the docks and waited. A few minutes later a white limousine pulled up near the *Elle's* ramp. Randi watched with interest as a man got out from the driver's side, walked around the back to the passenger door and opened it.

A pair of legs covered in white slacks stepped from the car. The slender woman stood wearing a matching white jacket and over-sized, black-rimmed sunglasses. Her long, dark hair shimmered in the sunlight as it fell down her back.

Without a backward glance to the man who'd opened the door, the woman strolled toward the ramp while he proceeded to pull several suitcases from the back of the vehicle. He followed obediently behind her and in minutes both were boarding the ship.

As the woman neared the top, Randi could see she was beautiful. She'd pulled her hair away from her face with a tortoise shell headband revealing a high forehead, and perfectly plucked brows framing a set of smoky-brown eyes.

So this was the lady joining the captain for the next leg of their journey. She reminded Randi of the women from her own social circle in Charleston. Palm Island Country Club was full of them.

Randi knew the type, having met her share at finishing school and beyond. Her own social standing dictated as much. She'd left the school with several lifelong friends and even though her experience had been a good one, she found most of the girls put on airs when they hadn't needed to.

This woman's regal carriage and feminine elegance would turn the head of every crewman on board, including the captain.

Speaking of... Noah strode toward the gorgeous woman, the look on his face far from pleased.

"Elaina, you're early. I'd planned to meet you on the dock."

She approached the captain with a glorious smile and outstretched arms, which he graciously accepted. It seemed to Randi his narrowed-eyed gaze revealed something other than cordiality. The woman approaching him had to be aware of it. Sure, she'd arrived a bit earlier than expected, but would Noah be put out by something as trivial as that? Not likely. Something else had to be going on, as the good captain was most definitely annoyed.

During the past few weeks, Randi had seen that very look in Noah's infuriatingly perceptive gaze. He'd directed it at her more than once since she'd been discovered. Maybe now she'd be spared those exasperating glances - at least for as long as the gorgeous Elaina was on the ship.

Elaina fluttered a well-manicured hand in the air as her delightful laugh trickled across the deck like pebbles skipping on a pond.

"It's all right, darling. Jeffrey and I wanted to beat the traffic."

Randi glanced over the deserted wharf area. Elaina was obviously prone to exaggeration.

Noah nodded to Jeffrey, then motioned for one of the crew to take Elaina's bags to her cabin. The dutiful Jeffrey said something to Elaina, shook Noah's hand, then departed.

Randi watched, intrigued, as the captain offered the woman at his side a pleasant smile. He then placed his hand to her slender waist and proceeded to guide her down the corridor to the reception area.

* * *

Noah entered the room with Elaina on his arm. He fought the sudden urge to tell her he was needed at the helm, even though the ship wasn't due to leave for another hour, and Jim was fully capable of handling the departure.

Her possessive clinging had never concerned him before, but now he found her behavior slightly uncomfortable. It didn't help that Randi followed close behind. He had no idea why her presence should bother him, but to have her witness Elaina's cloying attention was frankly embarrassing.

He glanced over his left shoulder and took note of the slight smile playing about Randi's mouth and her deep-eyed twinkle as she watched him. Instinctively he removed Elaina's hand from his forearm and quickly stepped to one of the chairs, pulling it out for her.

"Thank you, darling." With a flourish, Elaina took the chair.

"I've prepared shrimp remoulade salad and an assortment of pastries for you," Randi said. "Hot coffee and iced tea is on the sideboard. Let me know if you need anything else. I'll be in the galley."

"The flowers are lovely," Elaina said.

"Thank you. I had them especially delivered for your enjoyment."

"I think we've got it from here, Randi. You can go. Thanks."

"You're quite welcome." Randi flashed a brilliant smile and left.

Noah watched her leave. Head high, controlled and seemingly in her element. As if taking charge and serving others was second nature to her. Maybe she'd been a waitress in some high-end restaurant.

In the three weeks she'd been on board, he'd observed her, hoping to pick up on anything that would shed light on her real identity. He'd discovered she was bright and articulate and not at all afraid of hard work, making her failed attempt to run after a man like Phil Strong, out of place. Something about this entire situation just didn't add up.

He turned his attention to Elaina who stared questioningly at Randi's departing figure. "Since when do you hire female crew members?"

The hint of jealousy in her tone was unmistakable.

He picked up a crisp white napkin, flicked it in the air, then laid it across his lap. "I didn't. The crew was already in place when I decided to make this journey."

"I just wondered. She looks awfully young."

Something Elaina would notice. At thirty-seven, she was a gorgeous woman, but until this moment, he hadn't given much thought to her constant preening and obvious botox injections.

"What does she do on the ship?"

"Cleaning mostly and she's also taken cook's place. The poor man's malaria flared up and he left the ship two days ago."

"Well… this dish looks divine." Elaina forked a plump shrimp and placed it between her lips. "Mmmm, delicious."

"I'm glad you like it." He tipped his head, then lifted his wine glass to his lips.

"You seem distracted." Elaina reached across the table and placed her manicured fingers on his arm. "Is something wrong?"

"What? Oh, sorry. Yesterday there was an accident unloading one of the containers. I'm still trying to get my head around that. So. How was your flight?"

Noah tried his best to focus on Elaina's sparkling account of her travels, but his mind continued to wander.

Elaina's timing for a shipboard visit couldn't have come at a worse time. In hindsight, he wished now he'd nixed the idea when she'd first mentioned it months ago. The temptation to tell her to leave, as soon as she'd come on board, had been strong, but he knew he couldn't do that. She'd want an explanation and frankly, would deserve one.

The crew knew she was to be a guest and her sudden departure might alert the saboteur. At the time Noah had agreed to her visit, the voyage was supposed to be a routine merchandise delivery. Not an investigation into sabotage.

Under normal circumstances she would have been an enjoyable diversion. But with the container accident occurring one day before her arrival, her presence would only be an unwelcome distraction.

He sipped his wine and nodded at something Elaina was saying. Maybe her presence would take the saboteur off his guard. Speaking of distractions, there were now two women on board. He was curious to see how Elaina would handle that.

"Excuse me, sir." Pete stood in the doorway holding one of the ship's radios. "Chief needs to speak with you. Says it urgent."

Noah took the radio and pressed the talk button. "What is it?"

"You need to see this."

"I'll be right there."

"Elaina, I'll be a few minutes. Relax and enjoy your coffee. I won't be gone long."

Eight minutes later, he strode across the engine room floor. Eric stood inside the elevator entrance and when he saw Noah, waved him over.

"Show me," Noah said.

"I checked the signal integrity at the top of the elevator shaft. I also checked the communicating link between the controller and motor drive. When I pulled the shielded cable between the controller and the motor drive I found this."

Eric opened the metal panel to the right of the elevator door. The cable's rubber covering was stripped, revealing frayed wiring inside.

"This lift is ancient." Noah nodded toward the damaged wire. "Could that be the result of years of use?"

Eric shook his head. "This looks deliberate. See the clean edge on the cable? Had to be done with something sharp, like a knife."

Noah ran his hand across the back of his neck. "Can you fix it?"

"Yes."

"All right. For the time being, let's keep this to ourselves. Let me know when the lift is safe to use."

"Will do."

CHAPTER NINETEEN

Not long after the captain had left, Randi entered the ship's reception area. She crossed the floor to their empty table, wondering if his departure had anything to do with the elevator mishap.

Elaina was now seated alone in the outdoor dining room just off the officers' mess.

As quietly as she could, Randi quickly stacked the used plates and glasses, setting them on a tray. As she wiped the table she wondered what Noah saw in the woman, besides her long legs, small waist, and her perfect complexion.

About to make another catty, internal remark, she sobered, grimacing at her own stupidity. There was a time when others said the same kind of thing about her. She of all people knew what many saw on the outside rarely added up to who they were on the inside.

Stepping to the sink, she turned on the faucet and filled an ample amount of hot water over the stacked china. She soaped up one plate, rinsed it, then set it aside.

During her time as 'the talk of the Charleston social set', she too stood tall and long-legged in her spiked heels and designer dresses. Cruel things had been said about her. Hateful and most of them untrue.

Her response had been to put on her mask and take it like a true socialite soldier. She stared at the bubbles in the sink. The pain of those awful days sickened her even now.

"I brought you these." Elaina stood in the center of the galley holding a coffee cup in each hand.

"I'm sorry. I hope you haven't been standing there too long."

"Not at all."

"Let me take those. I'll pour you a fresh cup if you'd like."

"Don't bother. We're done. I saw you cleaning up and thought I'd help out."

"Thanks."

Elaina pivoted to leave, then turned back to Randi. "Would you mind stripping the sheets from my bed before I retire this evening?"

"I…put clean sheets on the bed yesterday. Is something wrong with them?"

"They smell a bit odd and the sink needs touching up and some fresh towels would be nice, as well."

Noah entered the galley and Randi couldn't help but wonder if Elaina's request had been timed perfectly for him to hear.

"Is there a problem with your stateroom?" He glanced from Elaina to Randi.

"Just a few minor issues," Elaina practically purred. "Nothing serious. Randi's promised to take care of it."

"I—"

"Miss Smith is an OS."

"A what?"

"An ordinary seaman. Or should I say, sea-woman. It's an entry-level job." Noah locked eyes with Randi's sending her an authoritative glance, which immediately turned to one of unadulterated pleading on his part.

So. Elaina was a pain in the good captain's neck. Good to know.

"I'll take care of it shortly," she said.

"Thank you, Randi." Elaina tucked her hand through Noah's arm in a possessive manner.

Randi seethed inwardly as they strolled back outside. What a hateful, manipulative woman. As if she didn't already have enough work to do. It was all Randi could do to stop herself from giving Elaina and the captain a piece of her mind right then and there.

Pleading brown eyes be damned.

But, common sense won the day. She bit her tongue and headed for Elaina's quarters.

As she suspected, all was in order. The bed hadn't been disturbed yet and even though the bathroom sink still sparkled from its earlier cleaning, Randi wiped it out anyway. Then took the one slightly used hand towel and replaced it with several more clean ones.

She was taking one last walk through when Elaina sauntered in.

Randi paused mid-stride. "I spruced everything up for you," she said, pasting on a smile. "Please let me know if I can do anything else." She sidestepped Elaina, but halted at the woman's next words.

"I figured you'd be here, so I thought I'd better check on my valuables."

"Excuse me?"

"You're a stowaway, which I believe makes you a sort of criminal."

So Noah told her. A twinge of disappointment flicked her insides. The captain was a lot of things, but she didn't think he'd stoop to idle gossip. So much for that pleading glance from earlier. She'd assumed they'd reached a sort of camaraderie, a mutual understanding, at least as far as Elaina was concerned, but apparently not. He didn't trust her and why should he?

"Randi Smith. Are you actually fool enough to think anyone believes that's your real name?"

Randi pressed her lips tightly together. Did Noah discuss her name, as well? "If that's all, I'll—"

"No. It's not all. I would appreciate it if you would not interrupt the captain and me when he and I are together."

"I didn't realize I had… Wait." Randi was the least snarky person she knew, but couldn't resist asking, "Are you jealous of an ordinary sea-woman?"

"Hardly."

"Then what?"

"I don't trust you."

"You mean you didn't expect another woman to be on the ship."

"Look at you." She waved her finely manicured hand in the air. "Broken nails, hair pulled up in a topknot, no make-up, wearing a man's clothes." Elaina shook her head with mock sadness. "A far cry from competition."

Randi forced a smile. "Well, I'm sure I could take more than a few pointers from you," she said, as she marched to the door. "But as you can imagine, as both maid and cook, I have work to do. Oh, one more thing…" Placing her hand on the door handle, she turned back. "You might want to keep in mind, *as* cook and maid, I have a key to every room on this ship."

Elaina's chest rose in fury. "Is that some sort of threat?"

"Of course, not." She smiled in earnest and closed the door. *Just giving you something to think about.*

Twenty minutes later, Elaina had already retuned to the captain's side when Randi entered the officers' mess to finish wiping down the last of the tables in preparation for breakfast. From the looks of Noah's creased brow, Elaina was most likely complaining… Again.

Randi watched as the woman offered a pretty pout, successfully manipulating her man, that is if the captain's placating response was to be believed. His efforts to soothe her were frankly too hard to watch. Was he really such a dope?

CHAPTER TWENTY

The following morning Randi got up extra early, hoping to get in her daily walk before breakfast. Her routine was to take a short mid-morning stroll before cleaning the cabins, but since the weather was supposed to take a turn for the worse she wanted to take her stroll now. She quickly prepped the galley for breakfast, then slipped out on deck.

The rule for anyone on board was to let a crew member know where you'd be on the ship. As a safety precaution no one took a walk without informing one of the crew first.

Unfortunately, no one was around except for Elaina who was lounging on one of the deck chairs. Wearing her dark-rimmed sunglasses and a yellow bikini, Elaina looked like she belonged on the pages of the fashion magazines stacked beside her.

Without any crew about, Randi would just have to take her walk later in the day. As she turned to go, Elaina waved from across the deck.

Most days since coming on board, Elaina skipped the formal breakfast, which meant Randi usually ended up bringing coffee to her cabin.

"I'm surprised to see you up this early," Randi said, as she approached her.

"It's way too hot for sunbathing later in the day."

Randi could well understand that. The temps were warm in this part of the hemisphere and the mornings and evenings were the coolest part of the day.

"But since you're here, would you mind bringing me a cool drink? Something long and fruity would be so nice. Oh and one for Noah, too, as he'll be joining me shortly."

On the verge of telling her to get it herself, she said, "Sure. Coming right up." *Your highness.*

She spun around and marched back to the galley. "Someone needs to tell her the *Elle* is not a five-star hotel." Randi huffed a sigh and jerked open the refrigerator door. She took out a half dozen oranges, then proceeded to squeeze the juice from them. She added a pineapple wedge on the glass rim, then emerged with two chilled glasses of fresh squeezed orange juice.

"There you go." She placed both glasses on the side table. "One for you and the captain. Enjoy."

Elaina took a sip. "This is orange juice."

"That's right. It's cold and fruity. Just like you wanted."

Elaina scrunched her nose. "You could have at least added vodka."

"Look. I'm sorry. This isn't the Ritz."

"Fine." She flicked her hand through the air in dismissal.

"Listen." Randi glanced at her watch. "I'd like to take a quick stroll but as you know, we're not supposed to do so without letting a crew member know where we're going. Would you mind letting the captain know where I am when he joins you?"

"Of course." Elaina waved Randi away with another flick of her wrist.

"I'll be on the starboard side."

A few minutes later, Randi paused near the railing to enjoy the view and the school of porpoises in the distance. As she gazed over the scene, a heavy breeze whipped her hair around her face. She reached into her jeans pocket and pulled out a hair-tie. Turning to face the wind, she deftly pulled the long strands up into a topknot.

As she turned to make her way back to the galley, an annoying creak and thump of metal against metal reverberated from somewhere nearby. She paused, turned left and continued toward the sound.

As she neared the center of the ship the banging abruptly stopped. She paused, listening – the whistling of wind between the stacked containers was all she heard. Then she saw it. A flash of clothing between the boxes.

"Hey," she yelled.

"Randi!" She spun around. Eric stood near the rail where she'd just come from and signaled her over. "We've been looking everywhere for you," he said.

Randi reached Eric's side, as he raised a walkie-talkie to his lips. "We found her. She's all right."

"You were looking for me?"

"Yes, we were worried about you. Especially Noah. And the men want their breakfast."

Randi glanced at her watch. "Oh dear. I'm so sorry."

Eric and Randi moved down the starboard side toward the deckhouse where several crew members were now dispersing. All except Noah and Elaina.

As Randi got closer, she cringed inwardly at the dark expression on Noah's face.

"I don't know what game you're playing, but no one takes a walk on deck without alerting a crew member beforehand."

"I know. I told Elaina—"

"Is Elaina part of the crew?"

Elaina stood several feet behind Noah wearing a smirk that clearly said she was enjoying Randi's discomfort.

"No."

"And what's the penalty for what you've done?"

"I lose the privilege."

Noah exhaled sharply as if he'd been holding his breath and lashed out. "My crew is hungry."

"Right." She gave a curt nod. "I'm on it."

She stepped around him blinking back the tears. She hated injustice and the sheer meanness of some people – and most of all, hated her own stupidity for trusting someone like Elaina. She'd been a fool to expect her to tell the truth.

Randi knew the rules. She should have alerted a crew member, but time was short and she wanted the walk more.

She entered the galley, turned on the stove and tossed a stick of butter in the stainless steel pan. This was her ship, for years her second home and to be denied a few minutes stroll on deck was hard to bear.

It wasn't like she was afraid of work, but being chief cook alone was a full-time job. The addition of cleaning all the cabins was taking a toll, both physically and emotionally. But she knew it was far more than that. It was the fear of losing the company, the thought of going bankrupt, and the heartache in her father's eyes. All of it terrified her.

She swiped at a tear, pulled the tray of eggs and hefty package of bacon from the fridge, then lit the stove focusing on the task at hand. That started, she checked to make sure her biscuits were rising, then attacked the large bowl of pancake batter.

Over the next few minutes, the mundane task of fixing breakfast kept her focused. Staying busy would get her through whatever came next.

Someone had opened a cargo box. She was certain of it. And after the accident in Sydney both were most likely connected.

Had the culprit known she was nearby? Elaina was the only one who knew where she'd gone and she was supposed to have let the captain know. But had she? And were the captain and Elaina the saboteurs? Or, was it someone else on board? And could Elaina be working with that someone?

She shook her head. Of course that was nonsense. Elaina had no part in it. Randi was rattled, that's all.

Just feed the crew, clean the galley, and get away from the captain's prying eyes.

* * *

Noah and the crew filed into the dining area, as Randi set out the last place setting. The whiff of bacon, fresh biscuits, and sausage filled the room with the fragrance of home. He hadn't breathed in the aroma of hot biscuits since he last visited his grandmother in St. Simons Island.

These were piled high on a platter in the center of the table. He knew his biscuits and from the looks of these, they were made from scratch.

As the officers and crew chatted about the upcoming day and impending storm, he turned his attention to Randi. She wasn't her usual animated self - unafraid to look him in the eye with the knowledge she knew something he didn't. Admittedly, he'd come to enjoy her forthright glances. Her open assessment of him and the others on board were nothing like the coy glances he received from Elaina.

He felt badly after this morning's confrontation. But his reaction had been more from anxiety than anything she'd actually done. And discovering the elevator had been deliberately vandalized only compounded the situation.

Had Randi been the target or was it simply an issue of being in the wrong place at the wrong time? He didn't know, but she'd been the one trapped on it and until he learned otherwise it was imperative he and Jim keep an eye on her.

There was a storm coming in less than twenty-four hours and the thought that she may have fallen overboard had terrified him. He shouldn't have laid into her in front of his crew or Elaina. He knew that woman and was fairly certain she'd delighted in Randi's dressing down. Randi had taken it on the chin, like a true sailor. And the crazy part? He'd respected her for it.

But looking at her now he could tell he'd upset her. He had no idea who she really was and he'd hoped the tongue-lashing and confinement would at least keep her safe.

Although a stowaway, there was something about her he found appealing. Truthfully, she fascinated him and he wanted to know more about her. Until now, she was pretty tight-lipped about her past and her identity. He was certain she was hiding something. And he'd swear on his life her name wasn't Smith.

He'd done a search on Randi Smith as well as other forms of her first name. There were way too many for him to fully vet. No matter. He'd find out eventually. Even if he had to follow her home once they returned to Charleston.

He pushed his plate away, then rested his chin in his hands. She was pouring coffee for some of his men and when she got to him he lifted his mug while she filled it up. "Thanks."

"You're welcome." She gave a curt nod.

Even though she'd avoided eye contact, he could tell from her misty eye, she'd been crying. A twinge of guilt squeezed his chest. He didn't know much about her but one thing he did know – Randi Smith loved the sea and everything connected to it. Noticed it when he was with her on deck or keeping an eye on her while she took her stroll. Saw it in her glowing eyes and slightly parted lips as if dreaming of something wonderful.

He sobered. It was the look of love. Phillip Strong came to mind. Could she be thinking of him when she gazed out over the South Pacific or up at the stars at night? That would account for those dreamy-eyed gazes.

An inkling of disappointment filled his heart and he pushed it away. Why should it bother him who she loved?

Later that afternoon Noah was in the middle of studying a chart when a knock sounded at his door. "Come in."

Randi stepped through holding the galvanized bucket of cleaning supplies and a mop.

"I wasn't expecting you today." He rolled up the chart. "I'll get out of your way."

"You're fine. I'm going through each cabin and cleaning all the bathrooms." Since I'm also the cook, I find breaking up the job this way is more time efficient."

"I see. Well, go ahead, then." He unrolled the chart, spread it on his desk and kept his head lowered as Randi strode past him into the bathroom.

As he studied the chart, the occasional slosh of water, and the clanging of metal bucket against tile, made him fully aware of her presence.

He glanced behind him. Randi was down on her hands and knees scrubbing the tile with a brush. He walked over, leaned against the doorjamb and shoved his hands into his pockets. He stood, chewing his inner lip, and watched her tackle the corners.

"My own mother never cleaned this well."

"I'm not your mother." Still on her knees, she scooted over to the next corner and attacked it.

"Working off some anger, are we?"

"If you say so."

She stood, wiped her forehead with the back of her hand, and stepped forward.

"Ah, you missed a spot."

She halted mid-stride, her head swiveling in his direction. Sparks of anger shot like darts from her heated gaze. She sucked in a breath and glanced at the floor. "Where?"

He took the brush from her hand and fell to his haunches. "Right here," he said, applying elbow grease to the spot. A minute later, he stood and handed her the brush. "All done and so are you. Leave the rest and come sit down."

"I have three more bathrooms to clean and dinner to prepare, so if you don't mind—"

"Sit. Down." He held her gaze until she finally relented.

She pursed her lips and stomped over to a leather club chair and sat. He pulled a couple of iced cold cokes from the miniature fridge in his office and handed her one. "You look like you could use a cold drink."

She took it from his hand. "I don't mean to sound ungracious, but since I have the responsibility for two jobs on board this vessel, I can't afford to dally."

"It'll only take a few minutes to drink your coke."

She took a long swig and glanced at him.

"See. That wasn't so hard."

She tipped her head back and took a longer drink. "So, am I supposed to thank you or something?"

"I'm not the stowaway."

"As you keep reminding me. And why did you have to tell *her*."

"Since there are only two females on this ship I'm assuming you mean Elaina. And what is it I'm supposed to have told her?"

"That I'm a stowaway. She's all but accused me of stealing her jewelry."

"Did you?"

"No, I'm not a thief."

"Just a stowaway."

"Yes."

He took a long drink and watched her. She appeared tired - gaunt as if she hadn't eaten in a while. Even in anger, her eyes mirrored concern and a touch of sadness. His gut told him she was no saboteur and he hoped to God he was right. She was too damned adorable for one thing, from her sweaty upper lip to the angry pout of her kissable lips.

Maybe she *was* in love with Strong or maybe just a lost kid trying to figure out her life. "Would you like me to send you home?"

Her eyes widened a fraction. "What?"

"I can, you know. I have the authority to get you home safely. No police. No arrest."

She licked her lips, and he couldn't help but wonder how they'd feel against his own. Beads of sweat still laced her perfect upper lip. A strand of hair that had come loose from her topknot fell appealingly along her flushed left cheek.

She took another long swig of coke, finishing it. Set the empty bottle on the low table near her feet, stood, then ran her hands up and down the side of her jeans. "I need to get going. Thanks for the drink."

She walked into the bathroom, gathered up the supplies and hurried out.

"You didn't answer my question," he yelled after her, but she'd already gone.

Noah twirled the coke bottle between his fingers. Everything he'd put her through the past three and a half weeks would make a grown man want to leave, but not her. She wanted to stay, which told him one thing… She was up to something and that something had to do with her cabin searches and with this ship.

He still pushed aside any thought she could be the saboteur. On one hand, it made perfect sense. She certainly knew a great deal about life aboard a freighter. Her familiarity with the ship was obvious and she pretty much had free range while on board.

On the other hand, there was the elevator incident. Could she have manipulated that to put him off the scent? Did she even have claustrophobia? He shook his head, unable to think of any other reason she'd want to stay. And until he did, he was back to square one.

Or, maybe she's a seafaring soul like you.

Chapter Twenty-One

The short stop in Melbourne to unload ten containers went off without a hitch. Once they set sail for Tasmania, Noah took a break to have coffee and dessert with Elaina - in hopes of managing her expectations.

She'd joined him on one other voyage in the past year. The trip took place on his family's newest ship from the Clayton Shipping Company. It had all the bells and whistles, including ten guest passenger stateroom suites, including wi-fi.

The *Elle* was an old soul, something Elaina would despise. He'd tried to warn her about the condition of the ship and had told her plainly it would not be up to her expectations, but she'd ignored his warnings – unfortunately, to her own discomfort.

"How long before we reach Tasmania?" she asked.

"Two days."

She rolled her eyes. "Can't you make this relic go any faster?"

"Cargo ships are much slower than a cruise ship. But, considering her age, the *Elle's* actually making good time."

She reached across the table and took his hand. "At least the company's first rate."

He gave her fingers a gentle squeeze, counting the minutes when he could get back to work. The saboteur could strike at any moment. One woman on board was distraction enough, but two? The safety of this ship and the crew were his responsibility. That should've been enough distraction for any captain.

"I'm sorry I can't spend more time with you. Maybe you should reconsider flying home from Hobart."

"If I wasn't fairly certain of your affection, I'd swear you were trying to get rid of me." She glanced toward the galley. "Careful, darling, or I might think you'd prefer a…younger, less sophisticated, type of companion."

"Elaina, you're a beautiful woman, and as such, jealousy doesn't become you."

"True, but so far, I haven't seen much to be all green-eyed about."

"That's where you're wrong." He shoved back his chair and stood. "If you'll excuse me, I have to speak with my *less-than-sophisticated* cook."

He didn't wait for Elaina's response. He left the reception room wondering what he ever saw in her.

Noah entered the galley and received a razor-sharp glance from Randi.

"Don't tell me. Was her highness's coffee cold, or was the cream not heated to her liking?"

He stuffed his hands into his khakis. Randi wasn't far off in her assessment of Elaina.

"I can see something's on your mind. So, out with it?"

She pulled on the corners of her mouth and shrugged. "Just that… she suits you."

That was the last thing he'd expected her to say. "What?"

She swung toward him and spoke as if explaining it to a child.

"She.

Suits.

You."

"What's that supposed to mean?"

"It means, you're perfect for each other," she huffed. "Two of a kind."

"Like two peas in a pod." He couldn't resist saying.

"Exactly."

He folded his arms and leaned his hip on the edge of the worktable. "In what way?"

Pivoting, she spun back to the sink and turned on the faucet. Her back rigid, she took her precious time squirting liquid soap across a mound of dirty china.

"You're both *extremely* opinionated, bossy, dictatorial... And basically," she glanced back over her shoulder, "all around annoying."

"That's it?"

She placed one of the plates on the drying rack. "I can continue if you'd like." She practically spat the words.

"That won't be necessary."

"Too bad." Wiping her hands on the front of her apron, she turned to face him. "I was just getting started."

He pushed himself off the table edge. "Speaking of getting started..." He strode to the far corner of the room, grabbed the mop, then held it out to her. "The floor is sticky."

She pressed her lips tightly together as her gaze burned into his. Mocking and challenging as only she could.

* * *

Noah had never enjoyed dinner less. Oh, the pork and lamb meat loaf, creamed chive potatoes and green beans were fine. The chocolate soufflé the best he'd ever tasted. But the burning sensation in the pit of his stomach ever since Elaina had informed him she was not leaving at the next port had given him more than heartburn.

Earlier, he'd pretty much insulted her and thought he'd at least have her *considering* a departure. But apparently, it backfired.

He turned his attention to Randi, who was at the opposite end of the table stacking used plates on a tray. Pete said something to her and she smiled, but it didn't reach her eyes. He couldn't blame her. She was biding her time until the crew had finished. She wanted to be anywhere but here. And he was sorry for that.

He dipped his head to his right and touched Elaina's hand. "I have some business to attend to. Let's meet for a nightcap in my cabin..." He flicked his cuff away from his watch. "In one hour."

"Of course," she purred. "I'd enjoy that."

Noah stood and motioned for Pete to follow him to the galley. Randi was in the process of setting shot glasses and tumblers on a tray.

"Pete, take over for Randi."

"Sure thing."

"Randi. Let's go out on deck. I'd like to talk with you."

As he stood at the door waiting for her, Randi set a glass on the counter, then followed him out. They'd only gone a short distance before stopping at the nearest railing.

She lifted her gaze to his with somewhat wary, questioning eyes.

"Relax. I just want to talk."

The black ocean barely reflected the sliver of light from the new moon. "I've noticed you seem to know as much about life at sea as this crew. That said, I know you wouldn't just willy-nilly break a rule. Eric said he found you in the middle of the containers."

"That's right."

"What were you doing there?"

"I heard a noise and went to investigate."

"What kind of noise?"

"Metal, creaking hinges, as if someone had opened one of the containers. And when I went to check, I saw someone."

"Who?" He gave her his full attention.

"I only got a brief glimpse. I couldn't tell who it was. But it was a man."

"Well, that knocks Elaina out."

Randi's lips quirked in a half-smile.

"Color of clothing? Anything to help identify him?" he added.

"Blue shirt and khakis. Crew gear. Nothing unusual."

"Okay."

She continued to look at him as if waiting for more.

"Not much of a view this evening," he said.

She glanced upward. "Except the stars shine brighter with less moonlight."

"True." A usual sight from the deck of a ship. Even though he never tired of it, he did sometimes take it for granted. But not her. His stowaway gazed on the whole scene as if it might disappear.

When had she become *his stowaway*?

"You look at it as if it's the last time you'll see it," he said.

"Do I?"

He nodded. "Why do you love it so?"

She sent a startled glance in his direction. "What, the sea?"

"Yes." He leaned forward placing his forearms on the rail. "All of it."

"Truthfully, I don't know. I suppose it's in my blood. My grandfather told me as much. I suppose he was right. I've always loved the ocean. Whether I'm on it like this, or looking at it from a beach. It draws me like nothing else."

"Like a lover?" he asked.

A dreamy smile parted her lips. "I suppose so. And I love ships. All kinds."

"And how is it you know this one so well?"

She stiffened, but only slightly - her hesitation subtle. If he'd not been watching her he would have missed it.

"Oh, you know. Once you've been on one, the floor plan of another is not that difficult to figure out."

"Is that so?"

She opened her mouth as if to speak, but didn't say a word.

"You never answered my question?"

"Which one?"

"The one I asked you before you ran out of my quarters." He held his breath, suddenly fearing her answer.

Her hands tightened on the rail as if weighing her answer. "I'd like to stay."

Relief flowed over him. "Good. Come on. I'll walk you to your cabin."

"What about Elaina?" she asked.

"What about her?"

"Won't she mind?"

"Would it matter to you if she did?"

"Not really."

"That's what I thought." He sighed. "Unfortunately, she's staying on longer than she'd originally planned."

"Lucky us."

He laughed. "Believe me, if I could figure out a way to change her mind, I would."

"I'll give it some thought," she said, as they reached her quarters. "Two minds are better than one."

Randi opened the cabin door and stepped across the threshold, then turned back to him. "Good night."

"Hey."

She paused. "Yes?"

"I'm sorry I made you cry."

"Oh." She shook her head. "It wasn't you…exactly."

"Elaina?"

She shrugged.

"Look, she's—"

"I can handle Elaina."

He quirked a brow.

"If you knew how many *Elainas* I know it would make your head spin."

"Then, I pity you."

A sweet laugh escaped her lips, followed by a genuine smile that lit up her face. His heart stopped, then beat frantically against his ribs. They'd shared a secret and in that moment he knew he'd like to share more than secrets with her.

"You can take your walk tomorrow, but I'm going with you. I want you to show me exactly where you saw that man today."

She nodded. "Good night."

"Night." Noah mulled over their conversation as he approached his stateroom. As he unlocked the door, a tender emotion squeezed his heart. A stowaway who speaks French and knows tons of *Elainas*. Randi Smith – you get more and more interesting by the day.

CHAPTER TWENTY-TWO

The next morning before Randi met Noah on the upper deck she tried her father's cell. She let it ring several times and worried when he didn't answer, she pressed end and dialed the house. Still no answer.

Randi found Noah patiently waiting when she arrived on deck. "Sorry I'm late. I was trying to reach my dad."

"Everything okay?"

"Yeah, I'm sure it is. Have you been waiting long?"

"Nope. I just got here."

They made their way in the direction Randi had taken the day before.

"This is where I was when I heard the squeak of metal. It came from over there." She pointed right. They proceeded between the containers and stopped about mid-way on the ship.

"Was it still open when you got here?"

"No. And I wasn't certain which one he'd tampered with."

He opened the container nearest them. A black Ford truck stared them in the face. He closed it, then proceeded to open the one to the right. Another Ford truck. This time, red. He opened two more in the same area. Both of those held kids' bicycles.

"There's nothing here anyone could steal. Except for a bike and it would be difficult to get off the ship unnoticed."

"Maybe it was just a curious crew member," she said.

"Maybe. Either way, I'll have the men keep a sharp eye out just in case."

"But it was one of the men that did this."

"And he'll know I'm on to him."

Noah left Randi to her duties and headed to the bridge. He'd announced the container slip-up to the crew, and hoped the saboteur would get the message and curtail his nefarious activities. Over the next eight hours, the crew would have enough to deal with preparing for the nasty storm heading toward them.

Thankfully, the rest of the day went on without incident. No clanging doors, nor fleeing crew members sighted by anyone.

Massive gray clouds rolled in over the ship and grew ominous, blocking out the setting sun. The oppressive heat lifted and the wind picked up with a steam of powerful gusts signaling the storm was near.

With the sea turning rough, a sit-down dinner would be too difficult to manage, so Randi had prepared a stack of hearty sandwiches with chips and fruit for the crew to eat when they could.

He and the men had long since secured the ship in preparation, so there wasn't much more to be done now, but wait. On the way to the dining room to grab a sandwich Elaina accosted him.

"Elaina. I thought you'd be safe and snug in your room by now."

"I will be, but after we've had dinner, first." She clasped his hand. "Come. You have to eat."

"Sure, but I'll have to make it quick," he said, as they entered the mess together.

They finished their sandwiches and Noah was on the verge of excusing himself, when Elaina leaned toward him offering a kiss. Out of the corner of his eye, he spotted Randi entering the dining room. He turned slightly and Elaina's kiss landed on the side of his mouth. Randi stopped abruptly, did an about face, and hurried out.

* * *

Right on cue, Noah stood and pulled out Elaina's chair. He'd never been more thankful for a storm-anything to put space between him and Elaina. And Randi's abrupt entrance hadn't hurt.

"The weather is only going to get worse," he said. "I'll feel better if you're safely in your cabin."

"You may be right." Elaina placed her hand over her stomach. "I'm not sure my sea legs will carry me through a major storm. How long do you think it'll last?"

"Through the night, I'm afraid. Doc will give you a transdermal patch if you need it."

"I'll be all right. Good night."

He watched Elaina go, then strode into the galley. Randi stood, in chief cook's red and blue striped apron, securing one of the cabinet doors when he entered. She snatched up a dishtowel, grabbed a plate and turned toward him.

"Sorry about that."

"No need to apologize."

"I'm almost done locking-down the galley. I only have a few more dishes to wash."

"I can see that." He leaned against the doorframe and folded his arms. "You've certainly figured out the system in your four weeks on board."

"And that's a problem?"

"No. On the contrary, I'm impressed. Especially since cook took ill and had to leave the ship in Sydney. I'm just wondering who taught you, that's all."

She briefly paused wiping out a mug. "Thanks for the compliment. It's not rocket science."

"Who says it was a compliment?"

Her hand stilled and she glanced over her shoulder. Turning slowly, she faced him. "Seriously, this is what you want to talk about when we have work to do?"

"See. That's exactly what I'm talking about. You know things. Ship things."

"That again." She twisted the tea towel between her fingers. "It's like I told you last night. I've always loved the ocean…ships…and anything and everything about them." She lifted a slender shoulder, and raised sincere eyes to his.

"And your interest and knowledge has me curious about you." *If she'd only open up with him. Tell him who she really was.* With any other woman he wouldn't care, but something about her brought out his tenacity. He stepped toward her, closing the gap between them.

Mouth gaping, she licked her lips and blinked. "Then you'll have to go on being curious, be…because there's nothing more to tell."

She turned her back to him, firmly setting the clean mug onto the shelf with a sharp thud.

When he didn't leave, she spun around. "I'm sorry, did you need something else?"

She had this knack of putting him in his place. Odd - considering her position on board. "May I remind you who's in charge here?"

"Right." Teeth clenched, she stared daggers at him. "I forgot."

"Do I also need to remind you of the penalty for mutiny?" She was even more beautiful when she was angry - regal and righteous as if she were the one in authority.

He tried to smother his smile, but failed. "Something tells me I should be calling you princess."

A telling twinkle appeared in her eyes. She shook her head causing the most delightful mess of tendrils to come loose from her topknot and fall over her cheek. She lifted the back of her hand and pushed the invasive strands off her flushed face.

"I… I'm hardly that," she stammered.

"I'm not so sure." He lifted his hand and tucked a loose strand behind her ear. "Finish up and secure yourself in your cabin. It's going to be a rough night."

* * *

Randi had no idea how long she stood there, hands on the mop handle, staring after the captain. The brush of his fingers along her temple had sent delightful shivers from her neck to her toes. His tingling touch made her stomach drop...and in a good way.

The ship rocked and pulled her back into the present. To heck with the floors. She placed the mop and bucket back into storage. With one final glance around the galley, she lifted her hand to her neck and shoulder, and gently massaged the areas.

What she wouldn't give for a massage and spa day. About half of the soreness in her lower back and neck had subsided since the good captain had forced her into manual labor. Until this experience she'd always believed she was in good physical shape and had taken pride in that fact. Apparently there were certain muscles immune to yoga and weight training. She pulled a face, firmly pressed her lower back, then flipped out the overhead lights.

Soon after leaving the galley, she realized she still wore the apron. As she turned to make her way back, the ship rolled and heaved. The front of the vessel dipped low as an enormous wave rose and crashed across the bow like a giant sea monster rising from the ocean floor.

Randi threw out her arms and planted her feet firmly on the deck. Elaina had to be miserable about now. She didn't like the woman but felt sorry for anyone who suffered seasickness.

As the ship surged forward, walking in a straight line was close to impossible. Arms flailing to the side - she moved along the deck like a drunken sailor. Staggering right, then left, doing everything in her power to maintain her balance.

She stumbled forward, then veered right as a gust of wind lifted her apron, flapping it in her face. Randi yanked the offending material over her head and as she did, the wind stripped it from her hands as she tossed it aside.

As she passed the first row of containers she heard a familiar grinding squeak. She stopped, straining her ears through the pummeling wind. Someone was actually screwing around with a container door. The ship swayed from side-to-side as she stumbled toward the sound.

She inspected two more rows, before spotting the box - its heavy door flapping like a flag in the wind.

Someone had deliberately left it open, knowing the storm would damage the contents.

As she approached the container, she glanced from side to side. The deckhouse lights glowed from the back of the ship. And except for the bridge, no one seemed to be about.

She wrestled with whether or not she should alert Noah, or seal the container, first. Whatever was inside could be destroyed if she didn't act now.

At that moment the ship rose on a huge swell of water, then lowered with a smack. Another massive dark wave engulfed the port side of the ship, spewing salt, sand and brine across the deck.

Randi froze and braced her body against the nearest container. Steadying herself, she placed her palms on the metal walls, then hand over hand, made her way to the open box.

Whoever opened it had to have left. No one in his right mind would be out here in this weather. But then again, maybe that was the point. The saboteur would know this -making the cargo an easy mark.

It would be impossible for her to memorize the twenty-digit box number, but she could at least check the cargo inside. She grabbed the metal door with both hands and pulled.

As she squinted into the blackness, a sudden, sharp, pain shot through the base of her skull. Randi saw stars. She tensed and clutched the back of her head, fighting waves of darkness as she slumped against a muscular frame.

The last thing she remembered was the firm grip tightening around her torso before she passed out.

CHAPTER TWENTY-THREE

Nothing like a storm at sea to keep one on his toes. Like turbulence to an airplane, raging seas came with the job. On a night like this every officer was on call.

Noah finished his watch at midnight, then left the bridge in both Scotty and Jim's capable hands. Once on deck 07, he continued down the hallway, shoulders bouncing from one side of the wall to the other, all the way to his room. Massive spray after spray attacked the *Elle* as a beast from the deep. A wall of wind and rain continued to pummel the ship, rocking her back and forth like a seesaw. Water was everywhere.

As he got ready for bed, he thought of Elaina. She had to be pretty miserable about now. It was too much to hope she'd changed her mind and accepted Doc's offer of a patch. Guess he'd find out in the morning.

Noah hit the bed fully clothed. He'd grab a few hours shut-eye, then head back to the bridge.

Several hours later, the ship rocked, nearly tossing Noah from his bed. That was a bad one. Fully awake, he glanced at his bedside clock. 5 a.m.

He brushed his teeth, then made his way to the galley for coffee. Once on deck the orange glow from the east signaled the storm would soon be ending. But, not so the waves. He knew from experience the rolling sea would continue for hours afterward.

Years at sea allowed him to keep his balance on the way to the galley. Once he poured himself a strong cup of Joe, he'd make his way to the bridge and relieve those on duty.

But when he got to the galley, the lights were off and there was no sign of coffee or bacon or anything else for that matter. Randi was always here by six, coffee made, and preparing her wonderful biscuits.

He flicked on the lights, then filled the carafe with water. While he waited for the coffee to brew, he wondered if Randi had succumbed to the weather. She appeared to have her sea legs well under control, but even the most experienced sometimes fell under Mother Nature's raging spell.

With a paper coffee cup in hand he made his way to her cabin. Outside her door, he took another sip and knocked. When she didn't answer, he knocked harder. "Randi." Still no answer. He unlocked the door, turned the handle and peeked inside.

"Randi. It's Noah. You okay?"

When she didn't answer, he entered the room. Her bed was made and the lights were out. Either she hadn't made it back to her cabin last night or she was up. There was only one way from her cabin to the galley and he would have passed her along the corridor.

He swallowed down the rising twinge of anxiety and left.

There was still no sign of her in the galley, so he tossed out the rest of his coffee and he headed to the bridge. He found Scotty at the wheel.

"Have you seen Randi this morning?"

"No. Last time I saw her was at dinner last night."

"If you see her tell her to wait for me in the galley."

Scotty nodded. "Sure thing."

Noah scoured the port side searching the deck and row after row between the walls of containers, until he spotted a blue and red mass of fabric at the rail base.

Randi's apron.

Fighting the unthinkable, he ran across the deck and picked up the wet, twisted wad. Clutching it, he stared, unseeing, over the ocean.

Dear God. Please, please, no.

The image of her falling, paralyzed with fear, being sucked under—

Desperation set his feet in motion. He sprinted to the bridge. "Stop the ship," he ordered.

"Sir?"

"You heard me, Scotty. Shut it down." He hit the ship's whistle with three prolonged blasts. He got on the horn. "Man overboard. I repeat, man overboard."

Jim entered the bridge, his face ashen. "My God. Who?"

"I can't find Randi." He held up the soggy apron. "I think she went over last night." Fear tightened his chest at the realization of what he'd just said. He fought back the desperation and the numbness that threatened to overcome him.

"Noah, you know what the result will be. You know it's too late."

"Turn. This. Ship. Around." Acute anxiety at what might have happened drove him to try and find her. "Too late" was not in his vocabulary.

"It could be a trick, to delay our deliveries."

"And you think she's a part of it? You think she's hiding somewhere onboard?"

"I don't know?"

"Exactly. None of that matters right now."

Jim nodded, placed a hand to Noah's shoulder and squeezed.

Noah left the bridge, unable to still his mounting anxiety and the horrifying thought she might have fallen overboard. Driven by the overwhelming sickness in the pit of his stomach, he strode back to where he'd found her apron.

Why would she have come out here? Randi was an able sea-woman and he knew for a fact she'd never risk her life unless…unless, she had to. Unless someone had forced her.

He swiped his hand across his mouth and tried to make sense of the nightmare. He darted through the rows. A sense of panic threatened to take charge of his emotions.

Why was she out here? Was Jim right? Had she been in league with the saboteur? And did something go wrong? Did they argue resulting in the unthinkable? He covered his face with his hands.

* * *

Randi moaned and rolled onto her back. Head pounding, she ran her tongue over her parched lips. Her neck throbbed. Sharp, excruciating, needles pierced the base of her head. Her stomach rocked with nausea. The night had been unbearable – frightening dreams, sleeping fitfully, dry heaves and more pain, until she'd prayed for it to be over.

It was all she could do to lift her eyelids. She stared into a pool of utter blackness. She gasped, strangling for air and fought the imminent fear.

Heart pounding, she lifted her hand to her face. She couldn't see it. Squeezing her eyes shut, she struggled against the rising panic in her chest. Fighting back dry heaves, she rolled to her side and pressed her hands to the floor. Hard metal seeped into her fingers. She was inside a container.

Her brain clicked over the events that ended up with her being shut in. She took a deep breath and pushed herself up. The metal ridges of the car pressed into the sweaty palms. She scooted back and rested her head against the container wall.

She lifted her hand and fingered the back of her head. The area felt sticky with blood. As she tried to make sense of what happened she focused on the immediate - getting out.

With shaking hands, she reached inside her pants pocket, pulled out her phone and checked the time. Six-thirty. She'd been in here all night. Using the light app she searched the container. Panic threatened to overwhelm her. What if they didn't find her?

"Get control, Randi." She spoke into the darkness. Hearing her own voice brought little comfort. Feeling faint, she closed her eyes against the unbearable heat – against the fear clutching her chest. *Stop. Stop it.*

She tucked her feet beneath her and stood, all the while keeping her left hand flush with the container wall. She turned the light until she found the door. Switching the phone in her left hand, she banged it with her right fist.

"Can anyone hear me? I need help," she yelled. She hit it several more times. "Heeeeelp!" A dizzying wave clouded her brain. She rested her forehead against the metal. "Please, somebody," she whispered.

* * *

As the ship made her way back to the location of the night before, Noah had every man available posted at specific lookout points. Scotty and Caffey stood watch on the wings. The rest of the crew took their positions, their faces serious and somber. Each one held a walkie-talkie for instant communication. The sun was now shining, but the seas were still rough from the storm.

Noah paced back and forth from port to starboard. Searching, searching, even though he knew it would be impossible to find her after eight hours. Lowering the binoculars, he stared out to sea, finally succumbing to the hopelessness that had long settled his chest and throat.

* * *

"Please." Randi whimpered and slumped against the container wall. Her shirt dripped with sweat and helped to keep her cool in the airless box. She sat back and tugged off her right sneaker, lifted it high in the air and hit the door.

Bang. Slap. Bang. Over and over.

"Somebody. Help!" She stifled a sob with her fist and fought for control - the extreme heat and the constant motion of the ship, about her undoing.

The inside of her mouth felt like cotton. Swallowing hadn't helped, either. Using the built-in flashlight, she pointed the iPhone into the belly of the container, hoping to find something, anything she could use to make noise.

Mostly boxes marked fragile and something yellow – near the center- a small car. She tripped and stumbled against a stack of cartons, then righted herself.

She clamored in the driver's side and laid on the horn, cringing against the deafening blast.

She stuck her finger in her left ear and pressed the horn again. This time she held it as long as she could stand it. The noise deafened. Tears coursed down her cheeks. Randi sobbed and pressed the horn again.

Chapter Twenty-Four

As Noah stood ready to call off the search, the muffled groan of a distant foghorn penetrated his thoughts. He turned toward the sound and lifted the walkie-talkie to his mouth. "Shut the engines," he ordered.

He held his breath and waited. There it was again. A car horn. Hope soared and he ran toward it. Scotty and Jim were nearby and headed in the same direction.

The three of them hit the rows, running in and out trying to get closer to the intermittent horn.

Noah skidded to a halt and listened. "Come on, Randi. Tell us where you are."

As if she'd heard his request, the horn blared loud and clear. Longer this time. Long enough to find her.

The three of them arrived at the container together. Noah grabbed the lever and pulled. The door opened flooding light into the dark cave of the compartment.

Then he saw her. Halfway back, head lowered, seated at the wheel of a yellow sports car. She squinted and lifted her tear-stained face to the light.

Noah was beside her in seconds. "My God, Randi."

He peeled her fingers from the steering wheel and pulled her in his arms. She was damp and hot and smelled of salt water. A sob broke from her lips and he tightened his hold.

"Shhh, it's okay. You're safe now. You're okay."

Randi trembled uncontrollably against him. She clutched the front of his shirt and buried her face against his chest. He held her and stroked her hair until her shakes subsided.

"Come on, let's get you out of here." He helped her from the car and led her to the edge of the compartment.

He hopped down, took hold of her waist and lifted her out. She collapsed against him and he scooped her into his arms.

"Scotty, have Doc meet me at her cabin and Jim, get this ship back on track."

Noah held Randi against his chest and strode across the deck. Her trembling body nearly broke his heart. At one point he wasn't sure if she clung to him or him to her. He gripped her tighter and she wound her arms around his neck as if he were her lifeline.

"It's okay, honey. You're going to be okay. I've got you. You're safe."

She wept softly into his shoulder. Once outside her cabin, Noah turned the door handle and carried her across the room. He gently lowered her to the bed, then propped her up with an extra pillow at her back. He quickly filled a glass of water and brought it to her.

"How's that?"

She took a long swallow, then lay back and swiped her cheeks. "Good," she whispered. "Thank you."

She shivered and he pulled a blanket over her. "Better?"

She nodded.

He pulled up a side chair and took her hand. "Doc is coming to check you out. What happened?"

She raised red-rimmed eyes to his, her cheeks damp with tears. The desperate plea in her wide gaze slammed him in the gut.

"Take your time."

"I was leaving the galley and I heard one of the box doors banging – over and over. I went to check it out and found one of the containers open. When I started to close it someone hit me from behind and put me inside."

"Did you get a look at him?"

She shook her head and lowered her gaze. "It was already dark, and I'd passed out. I don't know anything else."

She refused to look at him, just kept fingering the edge of the blanket. She'd resisted telling him more. Did she worry he had been the one who'd hit her? He'd have to rectify that - assure her she was safe with him.

One thing was certain, this incident proved once and for all, she was not the saboteur. But Jim's suggestion she could be in league with the culprit kept Noah in the cautious lane. Unlike the elevator, this incident was not a result of her being at the wrong place at the wrong time. This was intentional, an act of violence.

He took hold of her hand as someone tapped on the door. It was Doc.

"Randi." He approached her bed. "We're all so glad you're okay. I have to tell you we thought the worst."

Noah squeezed her hand. "We thought you'd gone overboard."

Her gaze flew to his, and she paled even more. "That's awful."

As the blood drained from her face, his boiled. Come hell or high water, he would find out who did this to her. It was one thing to sabotage a ship, but quite another to put someone's life in danger. She could have been killed. If they hadn't found her…

His gut tightened. First the lift and now this. Someone had deliberately locked her in a hot, dark, metal box for almost a day. Had he known about her phobia?

"Besides me, who else onboard knows you're claustrophobic?"

"As far as I know, no one. But it's not like I've tried to keep it a secret."

He stood. "Take care of her, Doc."

"You bet."

As he glanced at Randi, she pinned him with enormous, anxious, eyes. She had every reason to be afraid and most likely believed she had no one she could trust. It was suddenly imperative that she trust *him*.

CHAPTER TWENTY-FIVE

Doc gave Randi something to help her relax and then left with the promise to check on her later. She'd resisted closing her eyes as long as she could. The thought that someone could come into her room and hurt her or worse while she slept freaked her out. But Doc assured her she was safe. Apparently Noah had a twenty-four hour watch posted outside her cabin door and Pete was out there now.

She turned to her side and closed her eyes. As the medicine kicked in she found herself drifting off with the unsettling thought that Noah may have been the only person onboard who knew about her claustrophobia. The man who'd attacked her was strong and therefore most likely, young. She fell asleep thinking of Noah, how he'd carried her tightly and snugly in his arms – and he was most definitely young.

Randi woke with a start. The table lamp by the club chair shed a warm glow across the room. Light streamed in from the window telling her it was probably mid-afternoon. She sat up and leaned against the headboard.

Suddenly ravenous, she threw off the blanket and lowered her feet to the floor. Thankful her lightheadedness was now gone, she stood and made her way to the bathroom. She took a quick shower, then changed into clean clothes and headed out.

She found Noah, standing with his back to the door.

"Hi."

"Hi."

"It's good to see you up. How's the head?"

"Much better." She lifted a hand to the back of her neck. "I didn't expect to see you out here."

"It was my turn." He smiled.

It was warm and real and the kind that lit up his eyes and said he was glad to see her. She smiled back.

"I'm hungry," she said.

"Good. Me, too. I have to confess, I was hoping you'd wake up by now so we could eat together."

"Oh yeah?"

"Yup."

He took her hand and placed it on his arm for support. Support she didn't need, but found comforting all the same. It was nice to lean on someone, even if only for a few seconds. "So, who's cooking?"

"Chief. He's actually not bad. Oyster stew and French bread is on the menu. I hope that's okay."

"I didn't have to cook it so yeah, it's okay."

Once in the galley, he told her to sit. "I'll heat it up and serve you."

She wondered why he was being so kind. He probably had an ulterior motive. Ulterior or not, she'd enjoy it while it lasted.

She'd watched him with Elaina and knew he could be the perfect gentleman. She liked the captain and wanted to trust him. She'd have to lay her suspicions on the table, preferably now over lunch. The sooner the better.

She'd been on the *Elle* over four weeks now and still no closer to discovering the saboteur's identity. If she'd learned anything during that time, it was that she couldn't do this alone. Her plan had been to work with Captain Jack, but he wasn't here.

Noah was.

She prided herself as a good judge of character and her gut told her Noah was indeed that.

He ladled the stew into bowls, set them on the table, then seated himself across from her. They stayed silent on the first mouthful.

"What do you think?" he asked.

"I think I could be out of a job."

"Your job is safe. This is all Chief can cook."

Your job is safe. "You almost sound like you mean it."

He glanced at her. "What if I did?"

"I'd say you're a foolish captain, putting your crew at risk. You have no idea who I am. And if I were the owner of the Merrick line, I'd fire you."

The corner of his mouth lifted. "Like I said, you know way too much about ship life. So why don't you tell me who you really are?"

His lips curved into a to-die-for smile and she wondered how those lips would feel against her own. Sweet and sensuous? Crushing and demanding? Taking what she would only be too happy to give? She thought of the night when he'd held her against his chest. All strong and warm and capable.

She lowered her gaze to the bowl of stew. "I'm just a girl who got on a ship in search of a captain."

"And did you find him?"

She raised her gaze to his. What did he want from her? This change in his behavior confused and heaven help her...elated. She found it impossible to lower her gaze from his compelling one. "You're certainly not the one I expected."

"Right... Captain Strong." He huffed a sigh. "Forgive me, but I just don't see it. You and him."

She pursed her lips and shrugged. "I don't know what to say, I mean...love's a funny thing I guess."

"I guess."

They finished the rest of their meal in silence. As she stood to remove the bowls, he waved her back down. "I've got this. You're still recovering. Plus, Chief made dessert just for you."

"He did?"

Noah pulled two chilled bowls of mint chocolate chip ice cream from the freezer.

"He didn't make that."

"I know."

He placed a bowl in front of her and sat back down. "You do like mint chocolate chip, right?"

"I do."

"Something else I know about you."

"Speaking of things you know." She fiddled with her spoon. "Do you think whoever locked me in the container knew about my claustrophobia?"

"I've been wondering about that. The night I locked you in the brig, Pete was there so he would have heard most, if not all, our conversation that night."

"It wasn't Pete."

"How do you know?"

"Because the man who did this to me was muscular - strong. Average height, maybe. I felt his arms band around me, holding me to his chest before I blacked out." Her gaze traveled over his upper body as she spoke.

He glanced at his chest, then back at her. "You think I did it?"

She held his questioning stare for several long seconds. She had to ask. Had to put to rest her fears he might be involved with the sabotage ring. "Did you?"

Disbelief crossed his features. "No."

She nodded, gnawing her bottom lip.

He took his time stirring his coffee. "Does that mean you finally trust me?"

"I... I want to." *She so wanted to. Needed to.*

He reached across the table and placed his hand on her arm. "I want you to, as well."

"There you are, darling."

Noah retracted his hand as if he'd been burned. Elaina bursting onto the scene was like a douse of ocean water in Randi's face.

"I've been wondering where you'd gotten to." She spun toward Randi. "How are you feeling? I can't imagine what you must've gone through, locked up like that. Is there anything I can do?"

Even though her feminine voice dripped with sincerity, Randi knew from experience Elaina was all show.

"No. But thank you."

"Join us for coffee?" Noah asked.

"Love to," Elaina purred.

As Randi pushed her sore body from the chair, Noah stood and placed a steadying hand on her arm.

"Thank you for lunch. I might need some help with dinner this evening."

"Chief is already on it."

"Okay then. See y'all tonight." As she turned away, she could almost feel Elaina's glare at her back. She knew she had no right to feel rebuffed. It wasn't Noah's fault Elaina happened to come in the dining room just as things were getting interesting.

CHAPTER TWENTY-SIX

Saturday morning Noah got off the elliptical and wiped the sweat from his face with a white hand towel. He tipped the water bottle to his mouth and drank, then took a seat on the bench press. Scotty was perched on the stationary bike spinning away with a set of earplugs connected to his cell phone. The weight room was small, but well equipped.

About the time Noah had completed his third rep with the dumbbells, Pete ambled in dressed in a fitted t-shirt and gym shorts. For such a small man, he was quite the specimen - ripped arms, strong thighs and he hit the lat pull down like he owned it. Since Randi had described her assailant as muscular, Noah had made it a point to hit the gym more than usual. And from his observations half the men on the *Elle* were physically fit and any one of them could have knocked Randi out. He glanced at Scotty with his taut muscular torso – even him.

His workout complete, Noah made a b-line to his cabin. He'd planned to take Elaina into Hobart for the day, but wanted to speak to Randi before they left the ship.

Noah found her cleaning the reception room. "How are you feeling today?"

"Good, actually."

"Listen, Elaina and I will be spending the day on shore. I'm sorry you can't join us—"

She gave the wall sconce one more flick of the duster. "Seriously? Us?" She shook her head. "Thanks, but…"

"I mean it. I'd like for you to come, but without a passport that'd be impossible."

"As well as illegal." She stuffed the duster in the carrier and grabbed the mop.

"Exactly."

She rested the mop handle against her chest. "Don't worry about me. I have plenty to keep me occupied on board. Besides, you know me and ships. I'll be as happy as a clam."

That's what worries me, princess.

She gave him a sunny smile. "Have a good time."

"Thanks, I will."

Randi didn't seem the least bit put out that she'd be the only crew member who wouldn't be allowed ashore. She didn't know it, but he'd left someone behind to keep an eye on her. With specific orders for her to be *kept* under watch while he was gone.

Thirty minutes later, he and Elaina disembarked and once on the wharf he glanced back at the ship. Randi was leaning, chin in hand, on the rail watching him. She caught him staring, and offered a lazy salute that he could have sworn said, 'good riddance.'

Dream on, stowaway.

* * *

Randi held her position on deck while Elaina and the good captain exited the wharf via a yellow taxi. She waited a full minute after the car was out of sight, then made her way to Elaina's stateroom.

Her passport was right where she'd left it. She pulled it out from behind the picture and headed back to her cabin. Once there, she secured the document in her belted waist pack and got dressed.

She applied a bit of make up, which she hadn't done since boarding the *Elle,* then slipped her sundress and sandals into her backpack. She knew the captain would never leave her unattended, so she meandered about the vessel until she spotted the crew member. It was Chief and he was making his way to the opposite side of where she was standing. She waited until he disappeared from view, then headed to the off ramp.

With an occasional glance over her shoulder she hurried down the gangway to the wharf. She made a beeline for the nearest truck and hid behind its length until she felt safe to continue. Once off the dock, she headed for the nearest street.

She hadn't been to Hobart since Captain Jack had brought her here when she was fifteen. The color and magic of the place still enthralled her. In the distance someone played ancient tribal music from a didgeridoo instrument. Magical and hypnotic, the haunting strains reminded her of that first visit as she meandered through the streets.

In eight years nothing much had changed. The colorful Salamanca Market with vendors selling anything and everything reached as far as the eye could see.

She entered a local restaurant, ducked into the bathroom and then changed into her sundress. Afterward, she took a seat on the outdoor patio, ordered an omelet and a virgin pina colada, then settled back to enjoy the day.

She had no idea where the captain and Elaina were and hoped she'd not run into them. This day was hers – every delightful, sun-filled second, and she wasn't going to let anyone or anything stop her from enjoying it.

After weeks at sea, and coming no closer to discovering the culprit, she was ready for some R&R. She glanced at her hands. Once smooth and well-manicured, they now looked like she cooked and cleaned for a living. Which, amazingly…she hadn't minded at all. Next on her list would be a mani and pedi.

After the waiter brought her the tropical drink, she sipped the frozen deliciousness and gazed at her surroundings. Happy couples laughed and held hands, a small group danced on the grounds.

At the end of her second pina colada, she plucked the little paper umbrella from the pineapple wedge and sank her teeth into the sweet fruit.

Out of the corner of her eye she spotted a pair of white slacks. With the fruit still between her lips, her gaze rose up the urban Hawaiian style shirt into the dark caramel eyes of the captain.

Oops.

She slid the fruit fully into her mouth, chewed, then swallowed.

"May I join you?"

She gulped. "Y…yeah, sure." She glanced behind him. "Attila not with you?"

"Who?"

"The Hun. You know – haughty, proud, scourge of all lands."

"No, she's not." Noah took the chair opposite as the waiter approached the table.

"Something for you, sir?"

"I'll have what she's having."

"Right away."

"In case you hadn't noticed that lecher at the bar has been eyeing you for the past thirty minutes."

Her gaze widened. "You've been here that long?"

"Yes." The waiter set his drink in front of him and left. Noah continued to eye her as he took the first sip, then grimaced. "What, no alcohol?"

"It's ten in the morning."

He toyed with the straw and pinned her with his amber-eyed glance. "Okay, spill. How did you slip past Chief?"

"Easy. He went one way, I went the other."

"And Jim?"

"He was still on board? Somehow I missed that."

"Well, when he missed you, is when I got the call you'd disappeared."

"Sorry. Did I disrupt your outing with Elaina?"

"You do know you're breaking the law, right? If someone from the port authority asks to see your passport before you get back on the ship, you would be arrested."

She placed her lips on the straw and slurped up the last dregs of crushed ice and pineapple juice.

"I'm taking you back." He made a grab for her wrist.

"No way." She yanked her arm from his reach. "My day is just getting started."

She jumped up and headed for the exit. He slapped a large bill on the table and followed her.

"And I said, you're coming with me."

She spun toward him. "No, I'm not. I'm going to have one lousy day just for me." She stomped along the cracked sidewalk heading deeper into town, then stopped abruptly, turning toward him.

"I've worked my fingers to the bone for you." She shook her fist in his face.

"Whose fault is that? You're a stowaway. A law breaker. And if you get caught trying to board without a passport, you'll be in jail and trust me, no one here will care whether you have claustrophobia or not."

"Don't worry, I can safely get back on the ship."

"And just how do you plan on doing that?"

"I got on once before, didn't I? Right under that arrogant, perfectly chiseled nose of yours."

They stood staring each other down. Noah sucked in a breath and squinted against the mid-morning sun. Randi Smith was *the* most aggravating, impossible woman he'd ever met. Before he knew it, he'd grabbed her, pulled her against his chest and kissed her soundly on her mutinous lips.

"Fine. You can have your day, but you'll spend it with me. That way, I can keep an eye on you and can make sure you get safely back on the ship."

Mouth gaping, she stared - wide-eyed and unblinking up at him.

"I'll take that as a yes." He took hold of her arm and led her down the walkway.

"W…what about Elaina? Won't she be expecting you?

"You mean Attila?"

Randi burst out laughing. She glanced at him and was surprised by his smile. A crinkling at the corner, golden, honey-eyed, smile. Not that she didn't think he had one, but it quite mesmerized when directed at her. She knew somewhere in that stoic "me captain – you stowaway' attitude, resided a genuine sense of humor.

Unable to help herself, she grinned.

"She's having a spa day at the Savoy."

"So, she'll be coming back on board."

He nodded. "She's taking a taxi back to the ship this evening."

"I was hoping this was the end of the line for her."

"Me too."

Randi stopped and spun toward him. "Seriously?" She studied his face in case he was still teasing. But the uncomfortable, sheepish expression said otherwise.

"She was supposed to, but something or should I say someone… changed her mind."

"Hey, don't look at me. I want her gone as much as you do."

"Enough of her. I was out of line to even mention it."

"Don't worry, captain, your secret is safe with me."

At the next corner she spotted a walk-in nail spa. "Speaking of spas, I was planning to have my nails done today. Do you mind?"

"It's your day. If this is how you want to spend it, then don't let me stop you."

"How nice of you, sir."

"Noah."

They entered the salon and due to a cancellation were able to take her. She gave Noah the thumbs up sign, and he took a seat in the waiting area.

Thirty minutes later Randi stood in front of him. "What do you think?" She held her hands to his face.

"I think after a couple of days scrubbing pots and bathroom floors you'll have realized you've wasted your money."

"Sad, but true."

"Now what?"

"Let's go sit in a shady spot while they dry."

Chapter Twenty-Seven

Randi and Noah spent the rest of the morning visiting quaint little shops along the main thoroughfare, finally stopping for a late lunch at a little out-of-the-way café.

She glanced at her watch, uncertain as to what time the port authority closed and had to figure out a way to lose the captain so she could get there.

She'd written a letter to her uncle and hoped to somehow deliver it. Hobart, Tasmania was a popular route for the Merrick line and if her uncle arrived on one of their ships someone from the port authority could deliver her letter to him.

"That's the second time you've checked your watch. Do you have an appointment I need to know about?"

"Of course not."

She held his gaze hoping he couldn't see through her subterfuge. It was imperative she check with the port authority to see if any other Merrick ships were expected.

He shook his head. "Since you've come on board, you've yet to show your true colors."

"Don't you just love how some of our words and expressions have their roots from life at sea?"

"Like, *show your true colors*?"

"Exactly," she said.

"Here's one for you. *Ship Master*," he said.

"Sea Captain. A licensed mariner in ultimate command and authority of a merchant vessel."

"And don't you forget it," he said.

The definition had spilled from her lips as if she'd memorized it. Randi Smith fascinated him more and more. Without a doubt, he would certainly enjoy this day with her.

"Okay, Mr. Bossy. See if you know this one? *Plumb the depths.*"

He relaxed back in his chair, eyeing her. "Originally, it was a method to test the depths of the water. Now…. It means to fully investigate some thing or…someone."

"Namely me?"

"For a stowaway you're quite perceptive."

"And how's that investigation coming, Captain?"

"Still working on it, but come *hell or high water*, I will find out. And I'll continue to probe your identity until the *bitter end.*

"Hmm, the *calm before the storm*," she said. "Your attitude of doing whatever it takes may not only lead you to disaster, but painful disappointment. I'm surprised you'd take your search to such limits. Especially for a lowly stowaway."

"Careful, princess, or you might find yourself between the *devil and the deep blue sea.*"

"Are you saying I might end up in the unpleasant position of dangling over the side of the ship, caulking the devil seam?"

"I'm saying someone has to do it. In some cases it's the only way to keep the ship from sinking."

Suddenly this conversation wasn't fun anymore. It had gotten serious, reminding her of the danger in what she'd set out to do. And he spoke as if he too, were aware of it.

"I confess, that's one danger I don't care to face. I'm happy to clean and cook, but I draw the line at caulking the devil seam."

"Then you need to be careful. Because the way you're heading, you just might end up doing that."

His forthright stare told her he wasn't joking. Problem was, she wasn't quite sure about what. The attempts on her life? He didn't know the half of it.

He tossed down his drink. "What next?"

She licked her dry lips and took one last sip of her lemonade. "The lady who did my nails told me about a nearby bazaar."

"Let's do it." He shoved back his chair and stood.

Randi wouldn't dare check her watch again or he would definitely know she was up to something. They found the bazaar exactly where the salon lady said it would be. They'd shopped about fifteen minutes when she spotted the public restrooms.

"Hang here a bit. I need to use the bathroom."

"Okay."

At the bathroom entrance, she glanced back. Noah was scouring a table filled with mechanical parts. Keeping her eye on him, she snuck around the side of the building, leaving the bazaar behind her.

She hated to do it, but the port authority was only a block away, and if she didn't go now she might not get another opportunity. She just hoped it would still be open when she got there.

A few minutes later, she mounted the building steps and pushed through the brass-hinged oak door. Two redwood ceiling fans hung low, providing a welcome breeze from the tropical outdoor heat. An older man stood behind the oak counter, in front of an open file drawer.

"Excuse me?"

He turned toward her. "Yes, may I help you?"

"Would you mind checking to see if any vessels from the Merrick Shipping Line have been in port recently or due here in the coming days or weeks?"

"Let me check." He adjusted his eyeglasses over his nose and sat down at his computer. "It'll take a moment."

"Thanks." Randi drummed her fingers along the counter and waited.

Several minutes later, the man glanced up. "I'm sorry. I don't see any documentation of a Merrick Ship having been in our port other than the *Elle Merrick* and she's here now. Nothing else seems to be scheduled."

"Okay. Thank you."

The man nodded and went back to the file drawers stacked along the wall behind him.

Discouraged, Randi left the building. On her way out she tossed the letter in the trash, then made her way back to the bazaar.

The evening heat oppressed, making the trek back to the vendors seem forever. Ten minutes later when she still hadn't reached her destination, she realized she must have gone the wrong way.

She paused, made an effort to get her bearings, then continued until she finally saw it in the distance. A few minutes later, she eased her way into the vendor area and stopped at a table. She picked up a piece of pottery, examining it with feigned interest, all the while keeping a sharp eye out for Noah.

She strolled from table to table, meandering in, out, and through the vendors, but still no Noah. She checked her watch. She'd been gone almost forty minutes. Way too long for a bathroom break. Noah had most likely had it with her and gone on to other things. He would probably be angry with her for ditching him, but it couldn't be helped.

As she stopped at one of the tables she thought about her last call to her dad. When she'd pressed him for information about her uncle, he was evasive, but assured her Jack was fine. Which could mean any number of things. Someone could be sitting in a jail cell and be *fine*.

She wondered how the investigation was going from her dad's end. Carl Daniels was probably keeping it under the radar. It would be a disaster if the stockholders found out.

But why keep it from her? She'd felt totally in the dark. Lost.

After her dad discovered where she was, he hadn't seemed too worried about her. She thought it odd, but at least he'd stopped hounding her to return home. But not being able to reach him these past few days worried her.

She gazed around her surroundings. Speaking of lost... This was not the same bazaar she'd left earlier. That one was much smaller, and sat on a busy corner. No wonder it had taken so long to get back. And no wonder Noah wasn't here. She was in the wrong place.

She hurried right, then left, then straight ahead, finding herself in a sea of vendors, noise, and loud music. She made her way through the crowds until she hit a main road. Heavy traffic, car horns and throngs of people dotting the busy street.

There must be some sort of festival going on. She approached a street vendor and bought a pretzel.

Several rowdy teenagers jostled her as they hurried past. Randi ducked in an effort to avoid being hit, then headed down the street. She wasn't worried, but crowds had a similar effect on her as small spaces.

In dire need of direction, Randi made her way to a nearby bench, slid her backpack onto the seat beside her and sat down. Once she'd finished her pretzel, she approached a couple sitting on a neighboring bench.

"Sorry to bother you, but can you tell me which way to the Murray Street Pier?"

"Yes, it's about a twenty minute walk that way." The woman pointed in the direction behind Randi. "It's not the safest area, though. You might want to take a taxi."

She thanked them, then headed that way on foot. She'd grown up on and around docks. This one should be no different.

CHAPTER TWENTY-EIGHT

Noah checked his watch for the third time, then headed in the direction of the restrooms. Randi had been gone over eight minutes and the sudden thought she'd skipped out on him wasn't to be ignored.

When he got to the ladies room, he spotted a woman coming out.

"Excuse me. Did you happen to see a young woman inside? She's been in there awhile and I'm getting concerned."

"Sorry, no one but me. Maybe you just missed her and she's looking for you, too."

He smiled his thanks knowing full well he'd been duped. The bazaar was small compared to some of the others in town. He walked up the center aisle and when he didn't see her he tried to imagine where she would have gone.

He explored the immediate area without success, then expanded his search to the Salamanca Market. He covered several more blocks, but still no luck. He had half a mind to let her stay on shore. It would be no more than she deserved. And if, as she says, she can get back on board, then he'd deal with her later.

The sun would soon set and after his limited success on foot, he hailed a taxi and drove through the streets.

* * *

Randi gnawed her lower lip as she contemplated the deserted docks ahead of her. Either this was the longest twenty minutes of her life or she'd veered off course. She kept going until she spotted the crane lights from Hobart Port, then headed in that direction.

A few minutes later she hit the port railroad tracks. To her far right stacks of abandoned containers loomed with a sinister afterglow from the recent sunset. Ignoring them she turned left toward car lights and civilization.

Thinking about that couple's earlier warning she picked up her pace. Maybe it would be safer to approach the docks from the street instead of a container graveyard.

A terrifying screech ripped through the shadowy concrete walls. She jerked to a halt. A high-pitched howl followed by a series of low growls ensued. She tried not to panic as anxiety swirled in her stomach.

Two male cats flipped through the dark recesses from her left, landing at her feet. She yelped and staggered back. Gray and white fur flew from a mass of feline bodies as they screeched and growled in unnatural, ghostly moans.

She planted her right palm to her chest, let out a shaky breath, then ran toward the streetlights. Fear and adrenalin fueled her sneakers. She picked up her pace. As she was about to cross the narrow alley, a taxi careened to a stop at her feet.

Wide-eyed and breathless, Randi watched the back door open. Noah got out and stood facing her.

Thank you, God.

It was all she could do not to throw herself against his broad chest. At this point incurring the good captain's wrath, as well as his hot caramel gaze, was preferable to spending one more second in this place.

"You little idiot," he barked. "You must have half a brain to walk alone in this area after dark. I've been looking for you for hours. Are you *trying* to get yourself killed?"

"I...got lost."

"Was that before or after you ditched me?" Without saying another word, he motioned for her to get in the cab.

* * *

Noah's blood boiled. "Do you have any idea the danger you may have put yourself in tonight? As if I don't have enough on my plate without having to babysit you."

Randi stared at him with a tortured expression.

"I'm really sorry," she said. "I didn't realize—"

"No, you didn't." He shook his head. She was *the* most maddening creature alive.

"But you're right. I should've stayed on the main thoroughfare."

"You shouldn't have run off." He sucked in a deep breath. "You have no idea where you are or the trouble you could've gotten into. Kidnappers. Drug dealers. Human trafficking…"

He stared out the window. He couldn't say why, but his instinct to protect her burned in his gut. And after what he'd gone through the day before when he'd thought she'd gone overboard… If anything had happened to her… Jaw clenched, he inhaled and called upon some major self-control. He knew if he spoke again she'd come off the worst for it. He wasn't a mean person and he rarely lost his temper, but boy, oh boy, she was something else.

"Look, I'd only planned to be gone for twenty minutes or so. I got lost on my way back from…" She shook her head. "It doesn't matter where from—"

"Actually, it does. And you're going to tell me before this night is over."

They drove to the ship in silence. An abundance of blistering words rose to his lips, but he bit them back. Oh, he was tempted to continue, all right. But, what he wanted to say - what she sorely needed to hear - he'd most likely regret later, and her more so.

So he kept his mouth shut and his thoughts to himself. He needed time to cool off, and the ride back would give him that.

It was past nine when the driver pulled up to the *Elle Merrick's* ramp. Noah paid the driver and they got out.

Now that his anger had lessened, he was curious to see how Randi planned to get back on the ship.

"So, show me your stuff."

She glanced in his direction. "Watch and learn."

She seemed to access the situation, but didn't take immediate action.

"I'm waiting."

"Okay, I admit, this one's a bit trickier. Go stand over there and draw the inspector's attention away from the entrance, then I'll approach the—"

Noah threw her backpack over his shoulder, then scooped her up into his arms. She was light and firm and just for the heck of it, he tugged her even closer. She inhaled sharply and flattened her palm against his chest.

"What are you doing?"

"Shut up, rest your head against my shoulder, and pretend you're asleep."

"But—"

"Now. You watch and learn."

It surprised him when she did as she was told. Admittedly, her soft curves raised his pulse a notch. With her forehead tucked perfectly in the hollow of his neck, his desire to cradle her closer took hold, and he tightened his arms around her.

"You're too tense," he said. "You're supposed to be out cold. Relax."

Randi dangled her arm.

"That's better."

Noah approached the inspector. "Carl, it's—"

"Noah. How are you, friend?" He nodded to the bundle in Noah's arms. "Looks like you have your hands full." The man chuckled.

Noah made a point of looking at Randi. "More ways than I can count." He fought the temptation to plop this aggravating stowaway into the inspector's arms, right then and there. To rid himself of the extra burden of having her on board. She'd hate him for it, but this urge to keep her safe far outweighed any negative feelings she might have toward him. But the curve of her slender neck disappearing into the feminine folds of her colorful sundress acted the stop sign – bringing that idea to a sudden, screeching halt. "Um, I'd love to catch up but she's ill and I need to get her back onboard."

"Of course." Carl waved him on. "Hope everything's okay."

"Thanks."

Once Noah was on deck he glanced down at the woman nestled in his embrace. Eyes still closed, her lashes feathered like tiny fans along her cheeks. His gaze followed the line of her perfect nose to her full, slightly-parted lips, along her slender neck… His stomach dropped. An unfamiliar flutter tugged somewhere from deep within his chest. He cleared his throat.

"You can open your eyes now."

The tiny fans lifted, revealing her mild surprise.

"You know him? Why didn't you say so?"

For a moment he simply held her gaze. Should he tell her what he'd been thinking? Let her know how close he'd come to handing her over to the authorities? "I thought it would be more fun this way."

"For you maybe."

She continued to gaze at him, apparently without any thought to asking to be set on her feet. Which worked perfectly for him. As he had no intention of setting her down.

"So…from what the inspector said, I guess this means you *do* have a girl in every port."

Noah chose not to answer and continued down the passageway. Less is more. Let her think what she liked.

"Okay, you've made your point." She squirmed in his arms. "You can put me down, now."

"Sorry, stowaway, but you and I are going to have a little talk in the brig."

"I mean it." She pushed hard against his chest. "Put me down."

"In due time."

CHAPTER TWENTY-NINE

Not the brig…again. Panic rose in Randi's throat. Being cradled in his arms, snug against his chest was excruciatingly wonderful. A whiff of his after-shave weakened her at the knees, so it was probably a good thing she wasn't walking.

How could someone who smelled so wonderful be such a beast? Maybe she should try distracting him. His square jaw was one tiny, little, kiss away. All she had to do was lift her chin and place her lips on his and…

"I don't know who you are," he said, bringing her out of her musings, "but you're not leaving here until I find out." He set her on her feet inside the cell, then pushed the door shut.

She gripped the bars. "This isn't the seventeen hundreds, you know."

"Lucky for you it's not. Because if it was you'd be strapped over a gun barrel and whipped with a cat o' nine tails."

"And hung from the yardarm?"

"Of course not, in your case, a simple flogging would do."

He pulled up an industrial looking chair, and positioned himself in front of the cell.

She huffed out a sigh and placed her forehead against the bars. "Is this any way to end a really nice day?"

He folded his arms and held her with a stare. "Nice until you ditched me, scaring me half to death. I was this close," he lifted his hand and held his thumb and index finger an inch apart, "to leaving you to fend for yourself. You're lucky I found you when I did." He huffed out a sigh. "Maybe here you'll be safe." He ran his hand over the back of his neck. "At least I'll know where you are."

"Yesterday you thought I'd gone overboard. Where is that sweet, sensitive captain I've come to know?" She caught her bottom lip between her teeth, blinked and stared back. Maybe it was time she shot straight with him. Maybe if she gave a little he'd give something in return.

"That was yesterday," he said. "Why'd you sneak off?"

She hugged her torso and licked her lips. "I needed to check on something."

"How nice for you." His tone mocked. "Someplace, I take it, where I couldn't accompany you."

She glanced heavenward and sighed. "I went to the port authority's office."

"I see. And what exactly did you need to check on?"

"A shipping line."

"Don't tell me." He rocked back in the chair. "You're planning to stow away on another vessel, right?"

"No."

"Because if you're still looking for Strong, I could have told you his ship is nowhere near here."

She licked her lips and swallowed. "I wasn't looking for him."

"Who, then?"

She gnawed her lower lip, locking her gaze with his, searching his face for any sign he could *not* be trusted. His eyes still held a hint of anger from earlier, but also of something else. Worry. Concern. She wasn't sure if it was the intensity of his gaze or the fact that she couldn't spend another minute inside this cell. Either way, she had to make a decision and fast.

"Suit yourself." He unfolded his body from the chair. "No more of this cat and mouse game. You're staying put until you tell me everything." He spun on his heel and strode toward the door.

"Wait."

He came to a halt, but didn't turn around.

"Captain Jack. I was looking for Captain Jack."

There, it was out. Now let's see what he'd do with that information.

He turned slowly, mild surprise etching his handsome features.

"Go on," he said. "I'm listening."

She licked her dry lips. "I'm worried about him."

"Are you now? And how do you know Jack?"

She took in a steadying breath. "He's my uncle."

* * *

Noah had no idea if she was telling the truth, but the mere fact she knew the captain's name was hard to ignore. He stepped closer.

"What's Jack's last name?"

"Farthing."

"And is that also yours?"

"No. He's from my mother's side of the family."

She stared and wrapped her arms around her torso as if trying to stave off... Damn. He'd almost forgotten her fear of tight places. He quickly unlocked the metal gate.

She stepped through it. "Thank you."

"Don't thank me yet. This discussion is far from over. Come with me."

She followed him into the long corridor, then up seven decks to his office.

He allowed her to pass through first, then took a seat opposite her.

"So, is he all right?" she asked.

"You call your uncle, Captain Jack?"

She nodded. "Is he?"

"As far as I know."

"Why isn't he captain of the *Elle*?" Her father had told her one story. Let's see if it lined up with the captain's.

"It was the decision of the owner of Merrick Shipping that Jack be…temporarily replaced."

The third man in the library had thought so too and was the one who'd actually suggested it.

"Why?"

"For his safety."

"What do you mean?"

"I'm sorry, but I'm not at liberty to tell you any more." He had to tread carefully. The saboteur would most definitely know the name Jack Farthing and if she—

"Let's just lay our cards on the table." She stood. "There's a saboteur on board. You know it and I know it. So I suggest we work together to find him."

His jaw dropped. "How the— Did Farthing tell you?"

Her hesitation to answer was palpable.

"Yeeess."

"Why do I get the feeling that for you there's more to this story than the fact that your uncle was the ship's captain?"

"Merrick Shipping is my uncle's life. Ever since I can remember he's commanded one of Merrick's vessels. This vessel. My uncle and I are very close. Let's just say I know pretty much everything he knows. He loves the sea almost more than life itself, especially now that his wife is gone. Banning him to shore would destroy him."

"Spoken like a loving niece."

She spread her hands. "It's the truth."

"I'm almost convinced." At this point, he wasn't about to lay all his cards on the table. Her appearance on the *Elle* was far too coincidental. It was still possible her presence here could be a ruse, a distraction, simply to throw him off.

"Look. I have to trust someone," she said.

"And I'm that someone?"

"Yes."

He stood and stepped over to his desk and sat down. "As for your uncle, it's my understanding his situation is only temporary. Until some…things are sorted out."

"Things, meaning the deliberate attack on the *Elle Merrick*."

"You see. That's what I'm talking about. Your interest goes far beyond the wellbeing of your uncle."

"And if it does?"

"Another good reason for me to keep an eye on you, *Miss Smith*."

Chapter Thirty

Although this turn of events floored Noah, several things now made sense, whether she'd admit it or not. With her uncle as captain, she'd likely spent many days if not weeks on the *Elle*. And most likely over the course of some years. Her understanding of ship life, particularly on this vessel, was proof of that.

Noah retrieved his notebook from his desk drawer.

"Here's what I've ascertained so far."

Before he could speak further, Randi pulled a pocket-sized notebook from her backpack, then plucked a pencil from the captain's desk.

"May I?"

"By all means." He gnawed the inside of his lip and watched her flip through several pages before stopping.

"I'll go first," she said. "Here's what I have on the Chief engineer."

He held up his hand. "Wait. Just where have you gotten your information?"

"From spending time with him, searching his cabin, stuff like that. Admittedly, it's far from complete, but—"

"You searched his cabin?"

"Yes, his and the entire crew."

"I'm surprised you'd admit it," he said. "And the officers?"

She lifted a hand and scratched the side of her neck. "Them, too."

"I've kept you far busier than anyone else on board. So how have you had the time or for that matter how have you gone undetected?"

"Easy. When I clean the cabins I search them. Also, I took advantage of my alone time while you and the others went off shore."

"And me? Did you search here?"

She colored, and her gaze flickered to somewhere around his top button. "Yes. I...I also read your notes." She pointed at the book in his hand with her pencil.

"Then you already know what I've surmised."

"Some. I haven't had a chance to read all of it, as you already know."

He nodded. "Like when I caught you red-handed."

She dropped her gaze. "I noticed you didn't have a page on me, though."

"I'll be certain to rectify that. So," he kicked back in his chair, "tell me what you think."

"It can't be the chief."

"Because...?"

"Have you heard him talk about the engine room? He clucks over her like a mother hen. I can't see him doing anything to hurt the ship."

"It could be a ruse. A way to take us off the scent."

"I don't think so. It's a gut feeling."

"It so happens, I agree." He tipped his head toward her notes. "Who else?"

"Well, Pete..."

"Has a crush on you."

"You've noticed that too?"

"It's painfully obvious, I'm afraid. And I'd suggest, when the time comes, you let him down gently."

She flushed a pretty pink, revealing a side of Miss Smith he'd come to enjoy.

"What about Cook?" she said.

"He left the *Elle* in Sydney," he said.

"Are you sure?"

"I personally saw him off the ship. No way he could come back without anyone's knowledge."

"Of course he could and he could've also faked his illness. For all we know, he may be on board right now hiding somewhere."

"That's unlikely."

"I don't know." She tapped the end of the pencil against her right cheek. "If I hadn't needed sustenance I could have stayed hidden for weeks."

"Dream on, stowaway."

She shrugged. "Just sayin'."

"Who else?"

"There's Caffey and Scotty. I like them both and can't imagine them doing anything to hurt…uh, the ship."

A slip of her tongue. He steepled his fingers near his chest, wondering what she'd been about to say.

"They seem to be good and honest men. Truthfully, my one concern is Jim."

"Really."

"Yes. I get the feeling he's been watching me for weeks. It's rather creepy. And don't you find his familiarity with you odd? He acts like he's known you for years."

"That's because he's known me for years." He held her with his gaze. She stared back as if trying to make sense of what he'd just said. It was evident he'd surprised her. She licked her lips, swallowed and then dropped her gaze. At times her facial expressions were extremely readable and at others….

"Oh."

"*And* he has been monitoring you at my request."

"Well…" She lifted a finger and brushed a strand of auburn hair behind her right ear. "He's okay, then."

"He's okay."

"As for the rest of the crew…" She shrugged. "I don't know."

"Well, I do and like you I haven't anything concrete at the moment. Except for a few things I'm keeping to myself."

"Not fair. I just told you everything I know."

"That's doubtful. But at least one mystery's been solved."

"What's that?"

"Where your interest in ships comes from."

She blinked and gazed at him with some confusion.

"Your uncle."

"Oh, right." She nodded. "Of course. I spent many summers with him onboard the... his, um, boat."

There it was again. Aboard the what?

"During his breaks from sea, I take it," he said.

"Yes. He took me out often when he was home."

"Of course, being a captain he would have a boat."

She nodded. "I believe it was his family's. Sometimes my mother accompanied us."

"I see." *And I'd bet a year's salary you spent time on the Elle, too.* He leaned forward placing his hand on his chin. "She liked boating, as well?"

"She did."

Anything else?"

"She also enjoyed gardening."

"I meant on your list."

"Oh, no, nothing else. At least not at the moment."

"Someone tried to hurt you," he said, getting serious. "The fact your uncle was the former captain of this ship could be connected."

"You think the saboteur knows I'm related to Captain Jack?"

"It's very likely, and the reason you need to be extra careful. If I can't be with you, then Jim will be nearby." He stood. "But there's another possibility. But you're not going to want to hear it."

"Which is?"

"That your uncle could be involved."

"That's impossible."

"He knows everything about this ship. I understand he was once an engineer before becoming captain. You said it yourself. He lives and breathes the *Elle Merrick*."

"You're missing one important point. He'd never do anything to hurt me. There's no way he could be behind these recent attempts."

"You believe that?"

"I know it."

"Maybe, but either way, you'll continue to be under surveillance."

"Is it because you still don't trust me or because you think Captain Jack is involved?"

"I trust you, for now. And keeping you under watch is for your own protection."

"Look, since we're on the subject. I should probably tell you. Someone left me a note telling me to get off the ship. It was two weeks ago. Before that, somebody - most likely the same person - poured cooking oil all over the galley floor and I slipped and fell."

"When was this?"

"My first week here. Soon afterwards I found the note."

"Anything else happens, you tell me. All right?"

She nodded and stood. "If that's all, I'm for bed."

"I'll walk you."

"I'm just down the hallway."

"Okay. Listen. I don't want you on deck by yourself. Especially, at night. Understood?"

"Understood."

"Before you go," he said, "may I have my pass key back?"

"Uh, sure. It's in my pack." She reached into an inside pocket to retrieve it, just as he pulled open the pencil drawer at his deck. "But, I'll need it later when—"

"I believe this one belongs to you," he said, holding out her original key. "I'm assuming you brought this on board with you."

A crease formed between her gorgeous eyes, darkening them to the deepest blue-green.

"You searched my cabin?"

"Of course. After I checked the database and discovered there was no information on a Randi Smith, much less one ever having stowed away on board a ship, I had to carry out my own investigation. You were an unknown, and by maritime law, a lawbreaker. And as I am the law while at sea…" He shrugged, allowing her to fill in the rest.

They traded keys.

As she took the one from his hands, he said, "Your uncle's, I take it."

She opened her mouth to speak, seemed to think better of it, then nodded twirling the key between her fingers. "So you knew I'd been searching the cabins... But you said earlier—"

"I lied."

"I don't understand. Why didn't you stop me?"

"I was curious to see just how far you'd go." He perched on the edge of his desk and folded his arms. "The timing of your arrival, coupled with the fact I was on board to find the saboteur convinced me you were most likely the culprit or in league with him."

"I see."

"I need you to keep searching the rooms."

"Seriously?"

"Miss Smith, in dealing with you, I've found it's best to always be serious."

"Well... it won't be nearly as much fun, now that you know."

Chapter Thirty-One

The next afternoon, Randi mulled over the Elaina situation. They were due to dock tomorrow afternoon in Port Adelaide. There had to be a way to get her off the ship…get her to change her mind about staying on.

As she pondered the situation, Caffey clipped along the starboard side toward her and stopped.

"My cabin needs attention," he said. "If you would—"

"And as long as Willard, Jr. lives there, it won't be getting any from me."

"Well, he's gone. Escaped. I don't suppose you had anything to do with that."

"It wasn't me, but if you're saying he's gone, I'll take care of your quarters this afternoon."

"Thanks." He strode off.

In Randi's shipboard experience, there was always an occasional rodent to be found. A minor side effect that came with life on the docks. Truthfully, every crew member on this ship could have a pet rat if they wanted one.

As Randi watched Caffey push the elevator call button, an idea formed in her brain. An escaped rat was somewhere on the upper decks.

How convenient.

Randi cleaned the mess hall and galley in record time, then made her way below deck to the engine room. The ready heat inundated her body, giving rise to a thousand beads of sweat across her flesh. Who needed a sauna when you had this? She spotted the Chief at the far end.

"Randi, what brings you below decks? Everything all right?"

"Yes." She lifted her forearm to her brow. "How do you stand it down here?"

"With enough breaks up top, a body gets used to it. So, what gives?"

"I have a question."

"Shoot."

"Seen any rats, lately?"

"Do ducks like water," he said with a grin.

"I'll take that as a yes."

His smile suddenly faded and his eyes widened. "Don't tell me… you're with the health department."

"Nope, I just need a rat."

"The two-legged ones up top not good enough for you?"

She chuckled with a shake of her head. "Not for what I'm planning."

"Do I want to know?"

"Probably not." She shrugged. "If you did, you might be inclined to either stop me, or worse…report me to the captain."

"How many do you want?"

"One should do it. So, what do you say?"

"One wharf rat coming right up."

It was late when Randi entered her cabin. The men had stayed in the dining hall most of the evening playing cards and had asked her to join them, so it had been hours before she could clean up the place.

She kicked off her sneakers, and as she started to tug off her jeans, a knock sounded at her door. She snapped her waistband closed and stepped across the room.

Chief stood in the opening wearing a wide grin and holding a small, sealed, cardboard box in his hands.

"Sorry to disturb you this late, but I thought this particular *delivery* was best carried out after dark."

"Is that what I think it is?"

"Yup."

Randi took the box from Chief's hands. "Thanks."

He lifted a finger in salute and left.

As she closed the door she could hear the little devil scurrying around inside, its tiny claws scratching against cardboard. Her flesh crawled as she set the box on the floor.

Now that she had her universal key back, delivering one little rodent in the wee hours of the night should be no problem.

CHAPTER THIRTY-TWO

The following morning after he'd finished breakfast, Noah strode down the corridor to his stateroom. As he slid his key in the lock, he heard a scream. He spun left, just as Elaina burst from her cabin.

He was at her side in seconds. "Elaina, what is it? Are you all right?"

"That, that thing is in my room. A rat. He's enormous."

Noah blinked and stared. "Are you sure, I mean—"

"Of course, I'm sure." She huffed, angrily.

"Stay here, I'll check."

Noah walked through her quarters, glancing in and around the furniture. He searched underneath the bed, then entered the bathroom. As he pulled back the shower curtain, he spotted it. A dark brown mass, all fur and ears, huddled in the far corner, looking every bit as frightened as Elaina.

Noah stepped back, closing the bathroom door behind him. He found Elaina pacing in the corridor.

"Well?"

"I've shut him in the bathroom. I'll have Caffey take care of him."

"You'll do more than that. I want that man fired and put off the ship when we dock tomorrow."

"Hold on a minute. Are you suggesting he'd deliberately put a rodent in your cabin?"

"Who else, then. I've heard the crew talking about him having a pet one in his quarters."

"Even if someone deliberately did this, it's nothing but a harmless prank."

"Nothing? Harmless? I nearly had a heart attack."

"Look, I'm not letting him go, for you or anyone else. I have a minimum crew as it is."

"Then maybe it's time I leave." She lifted her manicured hand and brushed a dark strand off her forehead. "I can see this might not have been the best time for me to join you."

There it was - the manipulation. He'd wondered when she'd resort to that. In the past he would have tried to appease her, get her to change her mind, but not today.

"You're probably right. Why don't you relax in the reception room? I'll send Caffey to deal with your intruder right away."

All through dinner, Elaina's less than subtle attempts to get Noah to ask her to stay remained unsuccessful. Avoiding direct eye contact wasn't easy, as she seemed to pull out every piece of feminine ammunition available to her. Not that he was entirely immune, just that his interest was now focused on another.

The following afternoon, Noah stood next to Elaina at Port Adelaide, amidst three pieces of luggage while they waited for her taxi.

Certain he was being scrutinized, Noah glanced up at the *Elle*. Randi and two officers stood watching them from the main deck of the ship.

"I'll miss you," Elaina said, drawing his attention back to her. "But I can't say I'm sorry to leave this shell of a vessel. When I agreed to come, I thought you'd be commanding one of the Clayton Lines, as usual."

"I'm sorry your experience has not been as you'd expected. The change to the *Elle Merrick* was a last minute one, which I tried to explain to you."

"I know and I should have listened." She pouted prettily and wound her long fingers around his neck, pulling him in for a kiss. The taxi arrived and Elaina released her hold.

As Noah opened the passenger door, Elaina glanced up and scowled. Noah swiveled and followed her gaze.

The officers had dispersed, but Randi stood, right hand in the air, waving good-bye with a slight wiggle of her fingers.

Elaina frowned and slid inside the vehicle. "Until next time," she said.

He offered a smile, closed the back passenger door, and watched the driver pull away.

Once on deck, he turned at the railing and watched the taxi leave the wharf. Randi meandered over to his side and followed his gaze.

"Elaina's smile seemed strained, didn't it? No doubt a side effect of her recent introduction to Willard, Jr."

Dismayed, Noah eyed her in disbelief.

"You're welcome," she said, then sauntered off down the port side of the ship.

CHAPTER THIRTY-THREE

Randi took the dry bed linens from the dryer and set to folding them. She'd thoroughly cleaned stateroom one, happy to rid the room of Elaina's pungent perfume.

After putting the clean sheets away, she went down to the main deck to catch the last of the loading. As she pushed open the heavy outer hatch, she skidded to a halt.

Phillip.

Phillip Strong stood on the deck talking with Noah. How was this possible? Both Phillip and Noah turned toward her as if they'd sensed her presence.

She had to act fast. Keeping her identity secret depended on it. Adrenaline kicked in and she ran across the deck.

"Phillip." Randi flew at him and slapped his face, then whispered urgently. "*Follow along - call me Randi.*"

Phillip raised his hand to his left cheek and eyed her like she'd lost her mind.

"You told me you were the captain of the *Elle*," she said. "Explain yourself."

Phillip's jaw fell, and he glanced from her to Noah.

"I…I did…I mean…I was and then at the last minute I was assigned to the *Sans Merrick*. I tried to let you know, but you'd already left town."

"A likely story." She folded her arms and deliberately glared at him.

"Forgive me, sweetheart?" He drew her into his arms and before she realized what he'd intended, kissed her long and hard. As he lifted his head a tiny fleck of merriment sparked from his eyes.

She gave him her 'I'll deal with you, later' look and pulled out of his embrace.

Noah stiffened. "I'll give you two some time by yourselves." He turned abruptly and left.

"Okay, what's going on?"

"Come with me." She led Phillip to her cabin and once safely inside, turned to face him.

"What are you doing here?" he said.

"You first. Why aren't you on the *Sans Merrick*? Is she in trouble?"

"She's out of commission at the moment. I flew into Adelaide to get parts. Chief is with the ship keeping her afloat."

"Do you think it's sabotage?"

"So you heard about that."

"Of course."

"I thought your father had planned to keep you in the dark."

Seriously, did everyone know, except her?

"Oh, he tried. But that's why I'm here. I'm undercover. Even Noah doesn't know who I am. He thinks I'm Randi Smith, smitten with one Captain Phillip Strong."

"What?"

"You heard me. I told him I'd boarded the ship looking for you. Because of that, he's going to expect me to go with you, but under no circumstances can that happen. You have to think of a way to leave without me. And he has to believe it. He can't suspect a thing."

"Look, I've known Sheppard for years. I can't stand the guy, but you can trust him."

"Trust goes both ways. I'm not sure he's ready to trust me, yet."

"Okay, leave it to me."

* * *

Noah had just poured himself a drink in the stateroom when Phillip walked in.

"Where's Randi? I thought she'd be with you."

"Nope, she's um, meal planning."

"Would you like one?" Noah lifted his tumbler.

"Sorry, I can't. I have a ship that needs my attention, so I have to be going."

"Right.' Noah took a sip of bourbon. "I suppose you'll be taking Randi with you."

"About that. I told her I wasn't taking her."

"I don't understand, I thought—"

"I already have...how shall I put it...one female companion on-board. So..." he shrugged.

"I see—"

"Keep her with you or send her home," Phillip added. "I really don't care."

Noah saw red. He raised his fist and landed one on Phillip's jaw. Strong's hand flew to his chin as he stumbled back.

"Rescuing the fair maiden, as usual," Phillip said. "I'm sure you think I deserved that."

"You deserve that and more and in my opinion it's long overdue."

"I wondered when you were going to bring that up. We were in graduate school for God's sake. And your kid sister told me she was twenty. The only thing I'm guilty of is believing her."

"If it'd been the first and only time, then I would have."

"Can I help it if women love me— Take Randi for instance... Oh, my God. You like her." Phillip grinned.

Clenching his jaw, it was all Noah could do to restrain himself. "Randi is well rid of you. I just hope someday she realizes it," Noah said. "The sooner you're off my ship the better."

"Right, your ship. Now who's being duped?" He barked a laugh, then grimaced.

* * *

Randi paced impatiently near the off ramp with a hundred 'what-ifs' rolling through her brain. She could not leave this vessel. Not now.

Phillip strode across the deck holding his chin.

Finally.

"Okay, it's done." Phillip dropped his hand, then shifted his jaw back and forth.

"Oh, no. Don't tell me he hit you."

"Okay, I won't, but after what I said about you I could hardly blame the man. I feel like an A-1 jerk. He already thinks the worst of me, but now, thanks to you, I've sealed the deal."

"What do you mean?"

"Long story, sweetheart."

She offered a sympathetic smile.

"For what it's worth, I dumped you," he said.

"Thank you, Phillip. I owe you."

"Yeah, yeah. I just hope you know what you're doing."

"So do I."

* * *

Randi saw Phillip off the ship, then went in search of the captain. She found him in the chart room, standing at the sizeable square table, head down, examining a nautical map. The more modern vessels stored their maps electronically. The paper charts were old school and to some outdated, but as her uncle liked to say, *they work just the same.* And like her uncle, this was one of the things she still loved about the *Elle.*

She rapped twice on the door. "Noah." She crossed the room and stopped opposite him on the other side of the table.

She thought it odd when he didn't look at her. Without saying a word, he continued to examine the square sheet in front of him. The tilt of his head and serious profile was hard to read.

She shuffled from one foot to the other. "Are you okay?"

"Why wouldn't I be?"

Something wasn't right. She gazed at him, hoping for at least a glance from him. She was on the verge of leaving when he spoke.

"Don't expect your connection to Strong to get you any special treatment for the duration of this trip." He shuffled the charts, pulling another from the bottom of the pile.

Randi's jaw dropped. Totally and completely confused by his behavior, she glanced behind her. Except for the fact he'd mentioned Strong, she would have sworn he'd confused her with one of the crew.

Noah's lips pressed into a thin line as he continued to study the map at his fingertips.

She stood – one, long, painful, moment and stared. "I wouldn't have it any other way."

"Good." He put his back to her, pulled another chart from the cubbyhole and proceeded to unroll it.

She blinked back tears. "Sorry I bothered you." She pivoted on her heel and hurried out.

Pain squeezed her heart as she stepped into the passageway. What the heck just happened? She would've thought everything they'd been through this past week would have at least warranted a tiny little glance from the man. And if he'd believed the love of her life had just dumped her, wouldn't he have at least shown some inkling of sympathy?

She continued to mull over the situation as she made her way to her cabin. Sure, her presence had to be a royal pain for the man. She got that. But the six weeks on board, coupled with their day together on shore had to have meant something to him? She'd certainly felt it – the undeniable tug on her emotions, the longing to spend time with him on equal footing – to reveal her true identity.

He had no idea, but she understood him. His work, his love of ships and the sea. In that respect, she knew his very heart. Appreciated his abilities as captain. They were alike in that respect.

In her six weeks on board she'd never seen Noah this angry. What had Phillip said to him?

CHAPTER THIRTY-FOUR

Once Randi opened the door to her quarters, her nose twitched. *Gasoline.*

As she stepped cautiously into the cabin, the odor grew more pungent as she neared the bathroom.

A can of lighter fuel, cap off, sat near the sink. Someone had sprayed the fuel all over the counter and sink. To the right of the can, a note – neatly folded in half.

Hands trembling, she opened it.

Leave the ship while you still can or next time I light a match.

Fear squeezed her chest. Her muscles tightened. Phillip. Oh Lord, it couldn't be. She'd left him here when she'd gone to the galley. But he'd never do something like this. It had to have been someone else. Someone who knew she'd been occupied elsewhere.

She quickly washed up the area, keeping the fuel can and note as evidence. Pocketing the note, she placed the empty container in the cabinet underneath the sink.

For the second time since coming on board she was frightened. She gnawed her bottom lip. She should tell someone. The sooner the better.

The captain? Except he was in one foul mood. *Jim?* She sighed. The thought that she should have gone with Phillip peppered her brain. Too late for regrets.

She glanced at her watch. The crew will be wanting dinner. She hurried from the cabin, locking the door behind her.

Foul mood or not, she had to tell Noah.

Once in the galley she opened the utensil drawer and took out one of the smaller knives. She wrapped the blade in a paper towel, then placed it on the counter behind the sink.

Noah didn't show up for dinner. Scotty informed her he and Jim were on a conference call in the captain's office. Fine. She wasn't ready to face him, anyway.

Lucky for her, the rest of the men ate quickly. Apparently they were all excited about some heavyweight boxing match on TV. That worked for her. The sooner she could clean up and get back to the safety of her room, the better she'd feel. She'd promised the men her strawberry three-layered cake and left word with Scotty for them to help themselves.

"You're not joining us for the fight of the decade?" Scotty asked.

"Not my thing, but enjoy the cake."

"I'll take it in now."

"The plates and bowls are out and there's ice cream in the freezer."

"Everything okay? You don't look so hot."

"I'm beat, that's all. Enjoy the fight."

Ten minutes later, with the galley smelling of disinfectant, Randi turned out the overhead lights. With a quick glance behind her, she stepped over to the sink and picked up the knife. She gave the area a second look, then tucked the blade in her front waistband underneath her shirt. It wasn't much for self-defense, but it was better than nothing. Whether she could actually use it on someone was another matter.

The crew was already gathering for the fight when she passed the TV room. Minutes later, she entered her stateroom. She secured the door behind her, wedging the desk chair underneath the handle for good measure.

She should probably go look for Noah. But, after a second glance at the note she realized it was only a threat. No one in his right mind would start a fire while at sea.

The faint odor of lighter fuel still lingered when she entered the bathroom. She turned the shower to full blast, stripped off her clothes, then stepped underneath the hot water lathering up as much soap as she could to dispel the stench.

A soft sob broke from her lips, then another, until her salty tears freely coursed down the drain along with the smell of fuel.

* * *

Noah stood outside Randi's stateroom and knocked. He'd heard she'd left dessert for one of the officers to manage. Not that it mattered one bit, at this point he'd use any lame excuse to check on her.

His cruel words in the chart room hadn't set well with him. At the time, he was still dealing with his own history with Strong when she walked in, catching him off his guard. Admittedly, his anger at Strong hadn't been the only thing that had fueled his abrasive words toward Randi. The fact she still loved the man had angered him even more.

But, taking his feelings out on her was not cool. In fact, Strong's desertion had most likely hurt her. It shouldn't matter to him where Randi chose to place her affections, but it did. And for Noah to add to her pain was inexcusable.

He knocked again, then paused at the sound of furniture moving from inside near the entrance. A few seconds later she opened the door.

Randi stood hesitantly inside the opening wearing striped pajamas and a yellow robe.

"What do you want?"

The sound of her broken and husky voice pained him. "I wanted to see if you were okay." It was obvious from her misty eyes, she was anything but.

"That's not the impression I got this afternoon." She sniffed.

"I was angry. Yes. But not at you." It was a lie, but no reason to make her feel worse.

A hint of surprise flitted across her tear-stained cheeks. "Well, you could've fooled me."

"I deserved that, now may I come in?"

She blinked and lowered her gaze. For a split second he thought she was going to refuse, but with a curt nod she stepped back, opening the door wider for him to enter.

"Have a seat." She pointed to a chair, then she sat on the edge of the bed.

"Thank you." He eyed the desk chair near the door. "You rearranging the furniture?"

She followed his glance and shrugged. "I feel safer with a chair wedged at the door."

"I can understand that. With everything that's happened to—"

"Would you like a bottle of water?"

"No, I'm good. I'm planning to have coffee with a slice of your cake."

She folded her arms, took a deep breath, and stared at him.

"Come to apologize, then?"

"Yes."

Glancing down, she traced the pattern on her bedspread, refusing to look at him.

"I've upset you."

"What was your first clue?" She raised her chin and pinned him with a glare.

He bit back a smile. "The most obvious," he lifted a finger and circled his eye area, "your puffy, pink, splotchy—"

"I get it." She sniffed again. "And the least obvious?"

"Oh, I don't know. That's mostly intangible. A gut feeling – like the slump in your shoulders, skipping out during dessert, slinking off to bed earlier than normal."

"I'm tired, that's all."

"What's that smell?" He blinked and inhaled. "It's faint, but…"

"Lighter fluid. Sometimes I clean with it."

"Oh. Okay…well, I'll let you get your rest." He strode to the door and turned back. "Just so you know…he isn't worth it."

Randi lifted her head and stared. Lips parted and misty-eyed, she was beautiful. If she belonged to him, he'd have her in his arms this very second. Kissing her tears away. Making her forget there ever was a Phillip Strong.

* * *

"Wait."

Noah paused. "Yes?"

"There's something I need to show you." She crossed the room, snatched up her jeans from the back of the desk chair, then slipped the note from the front pocket. "Someone emptied a can of lighter fuel in my bathroom, then left this note."

He unfolded the paper and read. "When were you going to tell me about this?"

"Tonight before dinner. But you weren't there. I found it right after I left the chart room." She hung her head. "I should've gone back, but you weren't in a very receptive mood."

"It's my fault." He pulled her to him and wrapped his arms around her. "Forgive me, princess. I should never have unloaded on you like I did."

She closed her eyes and allowed herself to revel in his warm embrace, but finally pushed away, not quite ready to forgive. "What are we going to do about that?" She nodded to the note in his hands. "I didn't leave the ship like the note says. So, should we expect a fire in the next day or so? Or tonight while everyone's asleep?"

"I doubt it, but we'll have to stay vigilant - keep watch. Between Jim, Eric and me we should be able to monitor the ship. Make sure you keep your door locked when you're in your room."

"I took a knife from the kitchen. If I have to, I'll use it."

"Let's hope it doesn't come to that."

He gazed at her upturned face. "Are you all right, now?"

She nodded.

"Get some rest. I'll let the guys know what's going on."

CHAPTER THIRTY-FIVE

During the night, the ship passed through the Panama Canal on her way to Charleston leaving them five more long days to worry until they reached port.

Clean up came especially late this evening since the crew had invited Randi to take the captain's spot in the game, *Catan*. Deciding to leave the stack of dinnerware and cooking paraphernalia for later, she joined them. She glanced from one to the other as they drank, told jokes and poked fun at one another. It frightened her to think one of these very men had been the one to terrorize her.

It had been almost a week since she'd found the note and the lighter fuel and still no fire.

Jim, Eric and the captain seemed to be everywhere and nowhere the past week. As ones privy to the immediate danger, their vigilance was obvious to her. She'd also done her part with a watchful eye and her own surveillance. Since she'd been attacked and threatened by the culprit, it had been imperative she take great care as she went about the ship.

She figured Noah was standing post somewhere right now keeping a watchful eye out. She'd obsessed over the threatening note for days and Noah had been less social since she'd told him about it.

It was close to eleven when the game ended. She thanked the men and left.

An hour later, after clean-up, she shrugged into her warm sweatshirt, as the nights had grown colder since passing through the Panama

Canal. She left the galley with a hot mug of coffee for the second officer on watch. He thanked her and she left by way of the upper deck. The night was clear and the seas calm, a good time for a quick stroll.

About to pop back in to inform the officer on watch, she spotted Noah lying on the deck hatch near the bow. She hadn't seen him this quiet and still, much less alone, in almost a week. They'd not had one minute of privacy since she'd told him about the note and fuel.

As she stood watching him, she had to admit, Noah Sheppard, captain of her beloved *Elle Merrick*, was everything she'd ever dreamed of. Everything she'd ever wanted.

She still had no idea what Phillip had said to cause his anger, but she was nothing if not determined. Somehow she had to make things right. This strained relationship between them had to end. She'd found the man of her dreams and she wasn't about to let some misunderstanding ruin that. Still she hesitated, unsure if she'd be welcome.

The heck with that. She left the bridge, then strolled along the portside, staying near the railing until he spotted her.

* * *

"Randi." He sat up. "You looking for me?"

"I spotted you from the deck house and since it's such a lovely night for a stroll, I thought I'd say hi… And I told the man on duty where I'd be."

"Good girl. Come sit down."

The full moon and a single deck light shed a warm glow over the area as she took her seat next to him. She wore the same hooded sweatshirt from the night he'd captured her, reminding him of the feminine curves hidden underneath.

"It's gorgeous, isn't it?" She focused her attention overhead. "I never tire of it."

He gazed upward. "With no one but God, the sea and the stars for company, one gets used to it, I guess."

"I wish I could just bottle this night so I could have it forever."

She let out a contented sigh and gazed at the heavens, all dreamy-eyed and beautiful - the moonlight bouncing tiny sparks off her scarlet hair like fireflies in the night.

"Most of the women I know have very little interest in being at sea. But not you."

A sweet smile parted her lips and something close to shyness overcame her.

"Their idea of a sea adventure is the Ritz in Naples," he said.

She placed her palms behind her, leaned back on the canvas tarp and smiled her agreement.

"Since you…came on board…"

She glanced at him. "You mean, stowed away, don't you?"

Ignoring her, he continued. "I've had ample time to observe you. I realize I tend to focus on how much you seem to know about shipboard life. But, I just wanted you to know how much I admire and respect you for it. Your knowledge of the ship, your instincts regarding the crew…"

"It's like I told you before. When you love something you learn everything you can about it."

Which is what he was trying to do with her. Learn all he could before Charleston. *Then what? You're going to follow her home? Watch her fall into Strong's arms?*

"And how did you go about doing that?" There it was - her opening to share more, if she'd but take it. She still hadn't fully trusted him and part of his anger toward her that day in the chart room stemmed from that knowledge. He'd grown weary of her games and the added pressure of not having discovered the saboteur weighed heavily on him.

Her hesitancy was subtle, but most definitely there.

"Google has a wealth of information." Without moving her head, she cut her eyes in his direction.

"Right. Google." He shook his head. "Nice try, princess."

The corners of her mouth lifted. "I learned a lot from my uncle, of course, but also, by reading stories about life at sea. I have a library of books at home filled with such adventures. Historical accounts, especially ones about nineteenth-century women who lived aboard ships with their husbands."

"Hen Frigates."

She gaped at him.

He couldn't help but smile. "Don't look so surprised, maritime history is one of my favorite subjects."

"Most people never heard of the term."

"And yet a merchant ship with the captain's wife on board was a way of life for many seafaring families in the eighteen hundreds."

"Exactly."

She glanced back up at the stars and he took that moment to study her exquisite profile. A perfect silhouette against the moonlit sky. *Who are you, Randi Smith? You're like no other woman I've ever known.* "It's a special kind of woman who'd leave the comforts of land simply to spend months at sea to be with the man she loves."

She tore her gaze from the heavens and eyed him with keen interest. "And it's the rare man who refuses to leave his family behind."

Their gazes locked and held as a silent message passed between them.

"Sailing the seas back then was nothing like today," she said, breaking the silence. "The adventure, the dangers…"

"Romantic moonlit nights on deck," he said.

She colored adorably and stammered, "Seasickness…pirates."

"Saboteurs."

"Disease-carrying rats," she said.

"Unless it's Wilfred, Jr., of course."

She chuckled, sat up and drew her knees to her chest. "I used to love reading stories where the whole family lived on board. Adventures on the high seas always thrilled."

"Ever hear the one about Emma Armstrong and *The Templar?*"

Randi shook her head. "Tell me."

"Well, Emma's father was the captain and deathly ill. After surviving a heavy gale and yellow fever, which, sadly, took her mother and the lives of half the crew, Emma took charge of the vessel and navigated the ship along with the cargo safely into San Francisco's harbor."

As he told the story, Randi's face lit up like a child attending the circus. She gazed at him with such intensity he allowed himself to imagine it was toward him, but of course it was simply reaction to the tale.

"Amazing." Her eyes still riveted on his face, she asked, "What year was this?"

"It was 1879. But what's more remarkable was her age. She was fifteen."

An awestruck expression hovered over her upturned face. "Lucky her."

Although her reaction to the story seemed odd, even a bit unusual, it touched him deeply.

"Except for the yellow fever," he said.

"Except for that." She glanced down and ran her hands over the side of her jeans. "Thank you."

"You're welcome, but… I'm not sure what for."

"For reminding me what's important."

"Tell me?"

"Dreams and family. Doing whatever it takes to blend them together."

Was she thinking about Strong who'd left her high and dry? She gazed out over the ocean, pensive and thoughtful. Unable to help himself, he placed a finger to her chin, and turned her to face him. Even though her lovely gaze widened, she made no attempt to pull away. On the contrary, anticipation and desire flowed from her sparkling eyes.

"I thought you said I wasn't to expect any special treatment."

"Maybe I've changed my mind."

"It's not fair to change rules in the middle of a game."

"You think this is a game?"

"I don't know."

With his fingers still under her chin, he lowered his mouth to hers. She sat perfectly still, her lips warm and pliant against his. They sat on the canvas-covered deck hatch, lost in each other, the pungent sea air surrounding them.

* * *

Randi leaned in and wrapped her arms around his neck. Noah's strong embrace tightened along her torso, pulling her body against his. He lifted his head and ran his finger along her cheek. "Does that answer your question?"

Somewhat bemused, she nodded.

Her entire body tingled as she gazed at him with breathless wonder. Her previous relationships paled in comparison with what she felt for this man. In that instant she was totally and completely smitten with Captain Noah Sheppard.

No sooner had she realized it, he pulled away.

"What is it?"

"Strong."

"What about him?"

"He pretty much said you still loved him."

"He said that?"

"It was implied."

So that's why you were so angry in the chart room.

"Why should you care?"

Noah gathered her in his arms and kissed her, this time bringing her down on the tarp with him. This was more than a kiss - he was staking a claim – tilting her world on its axis. She breathed in his masculine scent, reveling in his strong, solid body, savoring every moment.

He lifted his head and placed a hand to the side of her head.

"That's why."

Warm amber eyes locked with hers. She entwined her arms around his neck and leaned against him. Noah ran his fingers through her thick mass of curls, reclaiming her mouth as he did so. Nothing else mattered except being in Noah Sheppard's arms.

A few minutes later, her head cradled in the crook of his shoulder, they lay side by side gazing up at the multitude of stars overhead.

"I've been thinking. Maybe we should introduce Phillip to Elaina."

His deep, wonderful chuckle escaped his lips. "It would be no more than he deserved."

"Seriously? And here I was thinking just the opposite. If you don't mind my asking, what happened between you two?"

"If it's all the same to you, I'd rather leave that one for another day."

Setting her curiosity aside, she buried her face in his neck and breathed in his clean masculine scent.

She thought about what her father would say when he'd discovered she would no longer be part of his upcoming merger. It was a good thing she'd not met the man, no telling what the introduction could have led to.

Noah pressed a kiss to the top of her head. "Tell me something. Did your father really try to force you into an arranged marriage?"

"Let's just say it was more of a suggestion."

"I'd say it was a lot more than that."

She raised her head a fraction and stared at him. "What makes you say that?"

"It was enough to make you run away in search of Strong."

She snuggled back down against him. "True."

"I don't know what's wrong with some of these men. If I had a daughter, I'd never try and force her to marry a man for any reason, especially my own gain."

"You say that like you've experienced it yourself."

"It's hard to believe, but I have."

"You're kidding."

"Nope."

She rose up to her elbow. "Tell me."

He eyed her, a slight smile playing about his lips. "A shipping magnate, who shall not be named, propositioned me to marry his daughter."

Randi felt the blood drain from her face. Her heart slowed as if she might faint. She blinked, her mouth suddenly dry.

"You okay?"

She nodded. "Yeah, yeah I'm fine. That...that poor girl." She swallowed. "Did you happen to meet her?"

"I refused. And lucky for me, she did, as well."

"Why lucky?"

"Apparently she didn't like the idea any more than I did."

"Oh."

"I saw a portrait of her."

"Pretty girl?"

"Hard to tell from the painting. Bleached blonde, unsmiling, nose in the air." He gave her his wonderful smile and tweaked her nose. "Not at all my type."

God help her, he'd just described Elaina and had put her in the same boat.

He pulled her back down beside him and hovered over her - a teasing twinkle in his eyes. "I prefer red heads," he said, sinking his fingers deep within her hair.

Tearing her gaze from his, she focused her attention on his shirt collar and swallowed. Noah tapped her chin forcing her to look at him. "What's troubling you, princess?"

"I..."

"Oh, don't tell me." He teased. "You dye your hair?"

She bit her lip and shook her head. "It's all me."

"So what is it, then."

"I've suddenly gotten tired, that's all. Five-thirty will be here before I know it and the crew will be hungry."

He glanced at his watch. "And I'm due at the bridge in fifteen minutes." He placed his mouth against hers. The warmth of his lips brought comfort to her confused heart. Although, quick and sweet, it held the promise of more to come.

He stood and reached for her hand. She grabbed hold and let him pull her to her feet.

They walked back to the tower in companionable silence. Companionable for him, anyway. She now knew the identity of the man her father had wanted her to meet the night of the gala. The man who had Captain Jack replaced. The man who had little respect for her father. And the man who'd pretty much told her she was not his type.

She realized then, he could never know. The fact that her father had tried to sell her to him was humiliating enough, but the thought he'd discover *she* was that woman, even more so.

CHAPTER THIRTY-SIX

Three days later, Noah sat at his office desk reviewing the inventory of the ship's cash and stores, when two taps sounded and Jim entered.

Noah straightened up. "Report."

"Everything seems fine. It's as if the saboteur disappeared or decided to quit."

"Don't believe it. We're less than two days from Charleston. Plenty of time for him to make a move."

"Doing what? We have no cargo. Everything's been delivered. We've even made up the time we took looking for Randi."

"Unless it's the ship he wants." Noah sat back and scrubbed his hand across his mouth. "His threats against Randi have been real enough, but I still haven't figured out why. Her only connection to all of this is Jack Farthing."

"Between the two of us we'll have to be extra vigilant," Jim said.

"Is there anyone else on board we can trust?"

"That's just it. I feel like we could trust any one of them."

"But we can't."

"I didn't say that. We may have to take our chances. It'll take more than us to keep an eye on Randi and stay alert for attempts at sabotage."

"Two reliable crew members should be enough."

"Okay. How about Eric and Pete."

"I get the chief, but Pete?"

"He has a thing for Randi. He follows her around like a lost puppy, so he may as well be of use. He can help keep an eye on her."

Jim left, and Noah went on his way to find Eric. He caught sight of him coming from the rec room.

"I just beat the socks off Scotty in ping-pong." Eric grinned.

"Just the man I want to see." Noah clapped Eric on his shoulder. "Walk with me a minute."

"This sounds serious. What's up?"

"Do you recall our conversation after the elevator incident?"

Eric nodded.

"As you surmised, there *is* a saboteur on board, and this time he left a note - threatening fire."

"Good God."

"I need you to be on the alert for anything out of the ordinary, especially in the engine room. Under no circumstance is anyone to be down there who's not supposed to be."

"Got it. Who else knows?"

"Jim." Something in his gut told him not to mention Randi.

"There's only twelve of us," Eric said. "Have you narrowed the field down as to who it could be?"

"Not as much as I'd hoped. Jim and I have been working on it since we left Charleston."

Chief nodded. "I'm glad you felt you could trust me."

Noah left Chief and found Pete chopping vegetables in the galley.

"Randi's not here."

"I'm not here to see her."

Pete set the knife aside and gave Noah his attention.

"You may have noticed that Randi seems to be the target of some... harmful jokes."

He nodded.

"Jim and I have tried our best to keep tabs on her, but it's near impossible. I'd like for you to keep an eye out for her. Will you do that?"

"Of course."

Noah rested a hand on Pete's shoulder. "Thanks. And let Jim or me know if you see anything out of the ordinary."

"I sure will."

"Oh, and not a word of this to Randi. I don't want her to worry."

"Yes, sir."

CHAPTER THIRTY-SEVEN

Randi woke up, nerves on high alert, as she showered and dressed. The *Elle Merrick* was scheduled to dock in Charleston after breakfast, which meant if the saboteur was to act, then he would have to do it soon. Even though there had been no additional notes or threats against her, she knew it was too much to hope that he'd given up.

She still held the note threatening fire in her pocket. Something about keeping it had helped her to stay vigilant.

Forty-five minutes later she set the sausage and biscuits in the center of the table next to the rest of the steaming hot breakfast. As the bulk of the men filed in and took their seats, she knew she'd miss this. Everything from their banter and good humor to their compliments on her cooking.

Once the crew settled in, she prepared a plate for Noah who was at the helm. He was by himself when she entered the bridge.

"I brought you some breakfast."

The ceramic plate was piled high with a hefty portion of scrambled eggs, bacon, sausage and biscuits.

"Mmm, smells great. Thanks."

While he ate Randi stood next to him overlooking the long, sprawling deck - now empty of containers.

"Is that Jim at the bow?"

He nodded. "And Scotty's aft."

"So, this is it, then."

"Yup. The checking procedure is complete and the crew assigned to their berthing stations. Once they finish breakfast, they'll take their positions. If you squint your eyes, you can see downtown Charleston in the distance, just beyond the pier," he said.

"I see it."

"Have you already eaten?" He broke off an ample piece of biscuit.

"I have." She watched him shovel a fork full of egg into his mouth. Even the good captain enjoyed her cooking. She knew it was a simple thing and rather silly, but she would hold on to this moment for a long time. The serenity, the camaraderie, the joy of being on board the *Elle*, and most of all the privilege of having been part of the crew.

"Thank you, Noah."

He glanced at her. "What for, princess?"

"For letting me stay. For asking me to be chief cook."

"What about having you clean the staterooms? You thankful for that?"

Even without looking at him she could hear the smile in his deep, wonderful, voice. A voice she would sorely miss.

"Yes, for that, too." She grinned and continued to watch the coastline grow nearer and nearer.

"So, um…you going to see Strong?" he asked.

She turned toward him. His previous humor was now gone and he stared at her with what seemed to her a multitude of questions in his gaze.

"Sure, I'll see him again." She sighed. "But not in the way you're thinking."

"What other way is there?"

"Oh, I don't know." She shrugged "Friendship? I could find him perfectly acceptable as an acquaintance. Couldn't you?"

"Not really."

The tugboats arrived along with the marine pilot who would assist the captain. After one of the tugs secured aft, the slow process of piloting the *Elle* through the harbor began.

"The tugs always remind me of *The Little Engine That Could*," he said.

She chuckled. "I adore the way they look. I had a collection of them when I was little – tub toys."

He smiled as he turned his attention from the instrument panel, to her.

"Will I ever see you again?" he said.

She thought about her father, his unfortunate attempt at match-making, and found it unlikely. She couldn't bear the thought of Noah discovering she was the bleached-blonde ice princess.

"I don't know." She did know, but no reason to be so *final* with him. She inwardly cringed. She should be saying *yes* or at least, *I hope so*. Or something coy like, *that's up to you.*

"Still keeping secrets?" He held her with his serious honey-gold gaze.

"Nothing that really matters now."

He gave a curt nod and faced forward, keeping his eye on the task at hand. When he didn't say anything further, she figured it was time for her to go. "Well, I'd better get packed. If you don't mind, I'd like to be here when you bring her in."

"Absolutely. You have about fifteen minutes."

She lifted to her tiptoes and kissed his cheek. "I'll be quick." She left the bridge with a lump in her throat. Even though his response had been pleasant, his cool attitude toward her spoke volumes.

* * *

The rest of Noah's breakfast tasted like cardboard. *She didn't know?* What the heck did that mean? He'd long decided to follow her after they'd docked. He couldn't let her leave without knowing how to find her again. But her admittance that she would see Strong again gave him pause. He would not run after another man's woman.

Had his reaction to her the other night simply been due to the stars overhead? The heady fragrance of her citrus-scented hair?

Her kisses had seemed real enough and, in those shared moments, he'd believed her response to him promised a future with her. But something had happened since that time and now.

He stepped right to check the radar and lifted his hand to his cheek. Her sweet kiss still lingered. As he surveyed the GPS screen, he heard a step behind him. As he glanced back, something hard clubbed the side of his head. A blinding light shot through his temple. He tensed against the needle-like pain, then slumped over and passed out.

* * *

The ache in Randi's heart grew as she put distance between her and the captain on the bridge. *Hold yourself together.* She stopped by state-room one, to retrieve her passport. Best to say focused on what needed to happen next or she just might bust into tears.

Once in her cabin she gathered her personal items and quickly tossed them in her knapsack. As she zipped the bag closed, someone pounded on her cabin door.

"Randi. Open up. There's a fire."

Oh, God. He'd done it. He'd started the fire. She sprinted across the carpet and yanked the door open.

Pete stood in the passageway with a gun in her face.

Her heart stopped, then thudded madly in her chest. She gripped the door jam and her knuckles went white. "Pete—"

"You're needed on the bridge," he said.

He took a step back. Her legs shook as she passed in front of him. "The crew—"

"The crew is busy," he hissed near her left ear. "Keep moving."

The beating ratcheted up a notch and now roared in her ears. She placed one foot in front of the other and moved forward. "Doing what?"

"Dealing with a distraction. The rest are at their berthing stations focused on their duties."

"And the fire?"

"That's a secret."

"You'll sink the ship."

"That's the plan, but we'll dock before that happens."

They turned right at the next passageway, then mounted the ladder to the bridge.

She glanced over her shoulder. "So, now what?"

"You're going to help bring this ship in. Then I'm going to get off and after that I don't care what you do."

They reached the top of the stairs and he pressed the gun barrel to the back of her neck. She flinched, sucking in air.

"Don't stop. That's just a friendly reminder."

She swallowed and moved forward. "You won't get away with this."

"I'll be long gone."

"The captain—"

"The good Captain is indisposed."

"What have you done to him?" Her voice shook.

"You'll find out soon enough."

"So, the elevator – the container… That was you?"

"Don't forget the cooking oil." He lowered the gun from her neck and grabbed her right arm.

Minutes later, they reached the bridge. Pete paused and motioned for Randi to enter. She spotted Noah on the floor bleeding from the side of his head. As she rushed to his side, Pete stepped through the door, then locked it behind him.

"Get up."

"Please. He needs help."

"He can have help after you bring the ship in."

"I…I don't know how."

He leveled the gun at her. "That's not what I heard…Miranda Merrick."

"You know who I am?"

"Of course."

All the pieces suddenly fell into place. His sympathy - his boyish charm – crushing on her – all an act.

"It's true," she said. "I have docked this ship. But only at my uncle's side." A total lie, but one she hoped Pete would believe.

He lifted the gun higher and pointed it at her face. "You can do it. I have faith in you, Randi."

Noah groaned from the floor.

"At least let me get Doc. It's one thing to damage the ship, but you don't want to be responsible for someone's death."

"You can have all the doctors and medics you want... *After* you dock the ship." His threatening tone rose an octave.

Self-preservation kicked in – if she pushed too far...

"Okay," she said. "But, I'll have to call the harbor master. I have no idea which pier and if I dock at the wrong one, they'll know something's wrong."

"Fine. But no funny business."

It was imperative Pete think she had no idea what she was doing. If she could *bungle* her way through the process, she might be able to convey an alert to the harbor master, leaving Pete none the wiser.

"I said do it."

"Okaaay."

Merrick Shipping had their own emergency code. If she could relay it... Seconds later she had the harbor master on the line.

"This is the *Elle Merrick*. The captain is indisposed and I'll be taking over.... That's right. Pier three? Thank you."

It took several minutes to maneuver the ship parallel to the berth. As the *Elle* made sideways, Randi checked the speed and the amount of drift.

She stopped the vessel and used the assistance of the tugs to finish the job. Any other time this event would've been a highlight for her, but Noah lay, possibly dying, at her feet. She shut the engines and lowered the gangplank.

"Let's go." Pete grabbed her arm.

"Wait. I have to sign off."

She'd kept the harbor master on the line as the *Elle* docked. Eyes straight ahead, she lifted the radio to her mouth. "Alpha-Six-Bravo-Seven. "That's correct. Alpha-six-bravo-seven."

Pete snatched the radio from her hands. "What did you do? What does that mean?"

"Nothing, I just followed protocol. It's the docking code," she lied.

Hoping to distract Pete, she glanced at Noah, lying deathly still on the floor.

Just as Pete followed her gaze, she took that second and slammed him with her full body weight. He careened left and landed on his back. She grabbed the radio.

"Mayday, mayday, mayday. This is the *Elle Merrick*. We have a fire on board. I repeat a fire on board. And a code blu—"

Pete put her in a chokehold. "Now you've done it." He cinched his grip even tighter.

Randi sank her nails into his forearm flesh. He cursed and released her, as a flare shot from somewhere along the port side.

She gasped and raised her hand to her neck. "Looks like someone found your fire," she choked out.

Two more flares soared through the sky.

Panicked and white faced, Pete glanced around the bridge as if trying to figure out what to do next. "You couldn't just dock the ship," he said, through clenched teeth. "You had to go and alert the authorities. Why didn't you leave when you had the chance?"

He grabbed her above the elbow. "Move."

She stumbled and fell against him as he unlocked the door.

"Why are you doing this?"

"You've heard the expression, blood is thicker than water? Well in my case it's congealing and way thicker than you or this ship."

"So you *are* working with someone?"

"Shut up." He thrust her ahead of him, the gun still at her back. "You're coming with me."

* * *

Noah moaned and opened his eyes. Nearby voices drummed into his semi-conscious brain. Squinting against the glaring lights overhead, he rolled to his side. Then reached overhead and grabbed the rim of the instrument panel.

Pulling himself to his feet took more effort than he'd first thought.

To shake off the dizzying wave, he paused and took stock of his surroundings. Through a hazy stare, he watched Pete haul Randi from the bridge with a gun at her back.

His heart stopped. He could not let Pete take her off the ship. Sucking in a steadying breath, he stepped forward. Light-headed and woozy, he stumbled onto the deck all the while keeping a blurred eye on Pete.

As he tried to make sense of the events taking place, he focused on the two departing figures. Somewhere inside he found the strength to run for it. He rushed forward and tackled Pete with both arms. They tumbled left away from Randi, hitting the deck in a tangled brawl.

In the scuffle, Pete dropped the gun. Randi swiftly kicked it across the deck. The men struggled until Pete slammed Noah into the bulkhead. Noah lost consciousness and collapsed on the deck giving Pete the upper hand. Like an avenging angel, Randi hurled an orange life ring at Pete's back, flattening him on his face just as the port authority officers boarded the ship.

Noah slumped against the deck railing trying to catch his breath. He sucked air fighting the raising nausea and throbbing pain in his head. Randi rushed to his side, knelt and gripped his right hand.

"The paramedics are almost here." She placed her hand gently to the side of his head. "You're going to be okay."

He lifted his left hand and pushed her tangled red hair from her beautiful, anxious face. Unfortunately, the paramedics chose that moment to swarm around him like bees to honey. He lost sight of her when they lifted him to the stretcher.

"Randi."

"I'm here." She hovered over him, forehead creased, her sparkling green eyes full of concern.

"We need to go, Miss."

She raised her gaze to the paramedics and nodded. As she stepped aside, Noah grasped her hand.

"You were amazing," he said.

Her gaze brimmed with tenderness and warmed his insides.

"So were you," she said, squeezing his fingers.

As the paramedics moved forward, he reluctantly released her hand, leaving him to stare at the clouds as they carried him down the gangplank and off the ship.

* * *

Randi stood on the wharf and watched the ambulance pull away. Even though she longed to go with Noah, the ship and crew needed her attention. Her insides twisted in all kinds of knots, just thinking of what could've happened here.

After the remaining crew had been released and the fire contained, the police began taking statements.

Now was not the time to let her emotions get the better of her. The fact that Pete had not worked alone, worried her. But first, she needed to give her statement to the police, and then go home to her father.

As she turned to make her way up the gangplank, the Merrick family Rolls Royce pulled onto the wharf.

Dad!

Randi hurled herself at John Merrick just as he stepped from the black luxury car. The comfort of his strong arms nearly had her in tears.

"Sweetheart. Are you okay? I came as soon as I heard."

Of course, the harbor master would have alerted him due to the emergency.

"I wanted to be the one to tell you. It's all been such a mess."

"I understand the police have someone in custody."

"That's right."

"I'm assuming he's the saboteur?"

"Looks like it."

"It's wonderful to have you home. Even though I knew you'd be safe under Noah's watch, I still had my bouts of apprehension."

She didn't want to talk to her father about Noah. Now or ever.

John Merrick placed his hand to his forehead and heaved a sigh.

"Dad, are you okay?" With everything else going on she hadn't noticed his pale skin and colorless lips.

"It's nothing. Fatigue."

"Sir, you should be back in your bed," Henry said.

"Dad, what are you not telling me? What's wrong?"

"Some liver issue." He threw up his hand. "Complete nonsense. Never had liver trouble in my life."

She placed her arm around her father. "Let's get you home."

CHAPTER THIRTY-EIGHT

It turned out the engine room fire had been nothing more than smoke and mirrors. Enough distraction for Pete to get most of the crew in one place. Once they'd entered Pete had simply locked them in. The police were now aware of the second person and assured her they would continue with their investigation.

Randi sat with her father, sipping a cup of tea, until he'd fallen asleep. She glanced at his bedside clock. It was only five-thirty - early enough for a visit to the hospital.

She gently closed her dad's bedroom door and spotted Henry in the hallway as she headed for her suite.

"How's Mr. Merrick?" he asked.

"He's resting. How long has he been like this? I thought he only suffered from panic attacks."

"Several months, I'm afraid. He didn't want to worry you."

"Too late for that." She glanced back at her father's room. "I'm going to shower, then head to the hospital."

"Miss. I hated to mention this while your father was awake, but there's something important I think you should see. It's at the Merrick docks."

"We just came from there a few hours ago. Can it wait until morning? I really need to get to the hospital."

"No, miss. I'm afraid it can't."

In the year he'd worked for her family, she'd never seen such a serious expression on Henry's face.

"You *know* something."

"To most who visit this house, I'm a fly on the wall. One can learn a great deal, when a mere insect."

"Let's go."

By the time they arrived at the wharf, the sun had set, leaving a remnant of orange and yellow ribbons pulling like taffy along the horizon.

Henry parked the Rolls and they got out.

"This way, miss."

They walked side by side through the walls of stacked containers, leaving the *Elle* behind them. As they traveled between the boxes, Randi began to sense an uneasiness.

"Are we almost there?"

"Not far now. Right up here to the left."

He casually took her arm. "This way," he said.

She stepped forward, then stopped at the soft click near her ear. Henry held a gun to her left temple.

Raw terror squeezed her throat shut. Blood rushed to her ears.

"Don't try anything stupid. I'd hate to destroy that beautiful face."

"You. Why?" she wailed.

"I'll get to that, but first… Take a look around you." He shook the gun across the containers. "All of this, everything you see should've belonged to my family – to me."

"I don't understand."

"When your grandfather was taking you all over the world aboard his precious *Elle* in your fancy little dresses, going to opera houses and attending five star dinners, I was visiting my father at the South Carolina Prison.

"While your grandfather wore fine tuxedos and business attire, mine spent his days in an orange jumpsuit."

"I'm so sorry, I—"

"It's too late for *sorrys*."

"Henry, you don't have to do this. I…I'm sure we could work something out." She stammered. "Some form of compensation for what you've lost. Please, it's not too late. You haven't hurt anyone yet. But if you do this—"

"Oh, but I have. You don't really think your grandfather's death was an accident, do you?"

Her heart seized as icy fear slid through her. "What do you mean?"

"Awww, you didn't know? Four grams of acetaminophen in his nightly bourbon and in a matter of weeks the deed was done. The fact he'd already suffered from cirrhosis of the liver hadn't hurt. He was dying anyway. I just hurried things along."

"You were on the *Elle.*"

"Chief cook at your service. Of course, I was a much younger man then." He gave a slight bow. The same arrogant tip of his head and shoulders she'd seen him use many times in her home. She'd always considered it overdone, if not a bit humorous, but now it screamed arrogance, mockery and deceit.

"I came on board the ship as Merrick's chief cook, the son of the man he'd ruined, and the old man didn't even recognize me. You were there, too. Dressed in your fine clothes, with the entire crew at your beck and call."

He circled her waving the gun in the air.

"Adoring, kowtowing fools. All of them." He snarled and got down in her face. "Even I played the part - making those tiny cakes and sandwiches for your tea parties."

She pressed a fist to her lips. Tears welled in her eyes and fell haphazardly to her cheeks.

"Don't waste your tears on him. His death should've been the end of the Merrick Shipping, but I didn't reckon on your father's business expertise and his ability to grow the company and make a success of it - the weak, sniveling…why he couldn't even look at a ship without getting seasick.

"So, I took another tactic – gain the trust of John Merrick and his lovely daughter. It took years, but it was worth it. My ultimate goal was to introduce you to Pete and somehow have you marry him, then I would have won. No muss- no fuss…

"But then you had to board the *Elle*. If you'd just stayed where you belonged.

"So. I had to revert to plan B. I gave Pete his orders, which he'd been willing to do. But what I failed to take into consideration was his attraction to you. Once he developed that crush, he refused to kill you. First time he ever disobeyed an order."

With lethal calmness, Henry plucked at a strand of her hair, sliding it through his fingers as he stepped behind and around her with the menacing stealth of a predator. "I can certainly see how you mesmerized him." He stopped and leveled his face mere inches from hers - his hot breath making her sick to her stomach. Repulsed, she reared back and twisted away.

He traced a finger down the side of her face sending snake-like shivers down her spine.

"Day after day in your house, seeing you in your finery…your priceless jewels, I too felt your undeniable pull."

As he ran his heated gaze over her form, her breath caught and held. Eyeing him, she tensed and stood perfectly still.

His eyes glazed over. "I can certainly see why he was so enamored with you."

Her breaths rippled out in ragged succession. In quiet terror she counted each second as if it would be her last.

He dropped his hand and stepped back. "Pete tried to get you off the ship, out of the way-to safety, but you wouldn't leave. I understood. You couldn't help yourself. You're tenacious, like your grandfather." He smirked. "I've had much better success with your father, though. He has no clue—"

"What do you mean?" Her voice wavered.

"It's a shame about his liver." His lips twisted into a cynical smile. "Apparently, that runs in your family, too."

"No." A wretched, sick feeling rocked her stomach. "We trusted you." The words tore from her lips.

"It pains me to do this. I like you. But it's time for you to go. And once you're dead, John Merrick will mourn you as he lays sick and dying."

If she could keep him talking… "Why the *Elle*? Why not one of our more modern ships. You could have simply executed a cyber attack on the navigation equipment. Crippling any one of them with a laptop computer."

"Because the *Elle* was the first. The one that started it all. The one my father invested in. As far as I'm concerned, the one that belonged to the Banes as well as the Merricks. Destroying Merrick Shipping through her is beautifully symbolic. Don't you think? But, enough chit-chat."

He nodded to the container next to them. "Open it."

Randi's hands shook as she grabbed the lever, pulled up and to the right.

"All the way."

Her hands still on the lever, she pulled the heavy door toward her, then glanced back.

Noah.

The captain stood several yards behind Henry, gripping a long piece of metal in his right hand. He lifted an index finger to his lips and continued stepping forward.

"Get in." Henry hissed the words.

"You don't have to kill me."

"I'm not. The container is. In a day or so, it's going to suffocate you, unless it drives you mad first."

A tremor snaked through her.

"Oh, yes. I know all about your claustrophobia. I understand Pete used it on you a couple of times while on the ship."

Noah stopped right behind Henry, lifted the iron rod and swung.

Henry grunted and sprawled flat out at Randi's feet.

Noah dropped the rod and was beside her in seconds. He gripped both her arms. "Are you okay? Did he hurt you?"

She shook her head. "How did you know I'd be here?"

"I didn't. I spotted the Rolls when I arrived. Since no one was around my gut told me something wasn't right, so I decided to check it out for myself."

"Why did you come to the dock?"

"As soon as I left the hospital, I came to check on the ship." He paused and held her with his intense gaze. "She may belong to you, but the *Elle Merrick* is still my responsibility - until John Merrick tells me otherwise."

"You heard all that?"

"Enough."

"For what it's worth, this is not how I wanted you to find out."

He pressed his lips together and stooped to pick up Henry's pistol.

"I'm sorry I didn't tell you who I was, but what I did tell you was the truth."

Noah stood, then stared right at her. "Really? Miss Smith?"

"Except for…maybe that."

He ran his hand around the back of his neck.

"I'd like to explain."

"Now's not the time." He grabbed her elbow and marched her to the car. "You need to get home to your father and call his doctor. I'll take care of Henry."

CHAPTER THIRTY-NINE

The Merrick family's household staff had been horrified to discover one of their own had turned out to be a kidnapper and murderer, and having lived, all this time, under the same roof with them. Mrs. Wayne had clucked over Miranda like a mother hen with her chick and proudly informed the rest of the staff that she'd always known Henry was a no-good-so-and-so.

Likewise, Mrs. Nelson had been appalled to discover Henry had used her to infiltrate the Merrick household.

As things began to settle down, Miranda became restless after having had the adventure of her life. The thought of everything going back to the way it had been before was unacceptable.

Even more disappointing, four weeks had passed without hearing anything from Noah. To fill her days, Randi decided to go ahead and take the two-week coast guard course for her captain's license. She didn't ask her father, simply told him of her plans.

Both Captain Jack and her dad attended the graduation.

"You passed with flying colors," Captain Jack said, kissing her cheek. "As I knew you would."

Flying colors – the phrase brought Noah to mind and their *nautical terms* conversation in Tasmania. Maybe if she'd showed her true colors sooner, he might be here with her now.

Randi sat on the brocade library sofa admiring the gold embossed certificate and captain's license in her hands. She was now qualified to master a ship no more than 100 tons and carry up to six paying passengers, as well. It wasn't enough to command the *Elle*, but it was a start.

Their dinner guests were due to arrive any time now to celebrate the upcoming merger of Merrick Shipping Line with the Clayton Company. Since returning home, she'd learned that Noah Sheppard was the owner of that shipping line. Disappointingly, he was not on tonight's guest list and most likely sent someone else from his company to represent him.

She couldn't blame him. He'd not been overjoyed to discover who she was. Yes, she'd deceived him, but had hoped he would have eventually understood why.

She laid the documents on the Queen Anne side-table, then picked up the latest copy of Yacht Magazine. The *Endless Summer* garnered the cover of the prestigious maritime lover's publication. She ran her hand covetously over the sleek lines of the fifty-foot vessel. As she did, a shadow fell across the page. She glanced back over the high-backed settee…

Noah stood behind the sofa gazing down at her.

"She's gorgeous, isn't she?" He held her gaze as he stepped around the end table to face her.

For a long second Randi could only stare at him. She swallowed and licked her lips. Speaking of gorgeous, Noah stood looking all manner of wonderful in a dark navy suit, with his hair neatly trimmed. Nothing casual-captain-like about him, but looking every bit the shipping magnate.

"Yes, she is." She set the magazine on the seat next to her and started to stand.

* * *

"No. Don't get up." But she'd already pushed herself off the seat, her evening gown swishing delightfully as she stood to face him.

God help him – Miranda Merrick's red-gold hair fell in soft waves around her beautiful face. Gone were the jeans, the blue Merrick polo shirt, her topknot and sneakers.

Instead, this shipping heiress stood before him an absolute vision in emerald green taffeta. The fitted bodice hugged her in all the right places, revealing soft, feminine curves. His gaze traveled to her slender waist, down the crisp fabric of her skirt, stopping just above a pair of sparkly heels.

He swallowed and lifted his gaze to hers, which held a hint of worried anticipation. Apparently, from her glistening wide-eyed expression and parted lips, she'd had no idea he'd planned to be here tonight.

Their gazes locked, and he couldn't breathe. Mouth dry he nodded toward the sofa. "May I?"

"Of course."

He picked up the magazine as they each took their seats, then tapped on the cover. "I happen to know the owner is looking for a captain."

"Oh, yeah?"

"Uh-huh. It so happens he's into maddening, red-headed, stow-aways."

She glanced down and camped her lower lip between her teeth.

"It's not like you to stare uncomfortably at the floor."

She nodded and seemed to fight back a smile.

"She's yours, isn't she?"

He nodded. "I don't suppose you'd have any interest?"

She raised her gaze to meet his. "More than you know."

"Oh, I think I do. Quite well, in fact. Your father told me you'd gotten your license."

"My father, huh? I'm surprised you'd have any dealings with him - in light of... everything. I'd watch your back, if I were you."

"Thanks for the advice. Anything else I should know?"

"He's a bit opinionated *and* manipulative, but in a completely, loving way."

"I'll keep that in mind." He fisted his hands in his lap. "I had a nice long talk with your uncle. He sends his love."

"I haven't seen him since I graduated." She brushed a loose strand of hair away from her forehead.

"I guess you know, he's back on the *Elle*."

"And happy as a clam."

"He told me all about you. Said you could dock a 200 million ton vessel with the best of them. And that he should know because he taught you."

She nodded, smiling.

"Only you would take that as a compliment. And it is."

"I admit. I was his star pupil…" She lowered her gaze and plucked at the folds of her dress. "I was beginning to wonder if I'd ever see you again." Her voice sounded shy, and uncertain.

"Truthfully? I wondered the same thing." It had taken him awhile to get his head around her true identity. Even now, seeing her dressed like a goddess… "I admit, I had some issues to work out."

"I'm sure you did." She stopped fiddling with her skirt and laced her fingers together. "I deceived you and—"

"No." He lifted his hand, stopping her.

"You don't need to explain a thing and you have nothing to apologize for. But you do realize, had I known your skill level, I would've made you my second officer." He teased.

Her lips parted into the sweetest smile he'd ever seen.

"Thank you. Hearing you say that means the world to me."

God, he'd missed her.

Randi Smith's transformation from steward/cook, to Miranda Merrick shipping heiress, would take some getting used to. As he gazed at her upturned face, he knew he'd enjoy every second of the journey.

"I brought you something." He pulled a small pink and yellow book from his inside pocket.

"My diary." Eyes shining, she took it from his hand. "I thought I'd lost it. Thank you."

"I found it on the ship a few days after Henry's arrest."

As she ran her hand over the cover, he added, "I took the liberty of reading it."

Her gaze flew to his. "You didn't."

"I figured it was only fair, since you read my journal."

She flushed the prettiest pink and shook her head.

"I learned a great deal about the young Miranda. How much she loved the *Elle Merrick*, her family, and the sea. I read about her dreams of becoming a captain. I would've liked your grandfather...and your mother."

"They would've liked you, too."

"I was touched by your last entry. I now understand *that* young woman." He glanced at her portrait above the massive desk. "You know," he folded his arms, "I think she's kind of growing on me."

Randi smiled. "Poor you, if that's the case."

She held his gaze with a sincerity that touched him, then blinked, breaking the spell.

"I...wasn't expecting you this evening. I'd assumed you would've sent a representative for the closing."

"Not a chance."

He took hold of her hands. "I've missed you so much. Missed your hands-on-hip, challenging, forthright glances. Your green-eyed twinkle when holding your many secrets. The way you worked without complaint - your chocolate soufflé."

She bubbled a laugh, then bit her lower lip and gazed at him with rapt attention.

"I needed to see you. Needed to know if you felt the same way about me as I do you."

A sweet smile peppered her mouth. "And what way is that?" she asked, breathlessly.

"I'm crazy in love with my stowaway. These past weeks—"

"Your...stowaway?

"That's right. Mine. And I have no intention of ever letting her go." Noah stood and pulled her to her feet. "Captain Miranda Merrick, will you marry me and sail the seas with me for as long as we both shall live?"

Miranda's brilliant smile told him all he needed to know.

"Yes. I will."

She stepped into his arms, then lifted her glowing face to his. His lips slowly descended to meet hers and Noah claimed them as any ship's master worth his salt would do - as if his life and future happiness depended on it.

Reluctantly, he raised his head. Randi gazed at him with all the love and adoration he could ever have dreamed of from his future bride - his stowaway - his love.

She entwined her arms around his neck and quivered against him. "*Shiver me timbers.*"

A deep laugh escaped his lips. "Sorry princess, but that expression doesn't quite fit in this instance."

"Speak for yourself. My legs are wobbly. Oh, I know. How about, *oh captain, my captain.*"

He hitched her closer, his mouth hovering over hers. "That's more like it."

Thank you for reading!

Dear Reader,

I hope you enjoyed **Stowaway**. I have to tell you, I really love the characters of Miranda and Noah. Though many readers wrote me asking, "What's next for Phillip?" Well, stay tuned, because Phillip's journey is not over and I guarantee he'll find his happy ending.

As an author, I love connecting with my readers. You can write me at darcyflynnromances@gmail.com and visit me on the web at www.darcyflynnromances.com. For occasional news sign up for my News Letter here: https://bit.ly/2CXlppI

Finally, I need to ask a favor. As you probably know, reviews can be hard to come by. And as a reader your feedback is so important. If you're so inclined, I'd be grateful for a review of **Stowaway**. It doesn't have to be long or fancy. :) One or two sentences is fine.

If you have time, here's a link to my author page on Amazon. You can check out all my books here:

http://www.amazon.com/-/e/B0077AG3ZM

Thank you so much for reading **Stowaway** and for spending time with me.

In gratitude,

Darcy Flynn

ABOUT THE AUTHOR

Award-Winning Author Darcy Flynn is known for her heartwarming, sweet contemporary romances. Her refreshing storylines, irritatingly handsome heroes and feisty heroines will delight and entertain you from the first page to the last. Miss Flynn's heroes and heroines have a tangible chemistry that is entertaining, humorous and competitive.

Darcy lives with her husband and a menagerie of other living creatures on her horse farm in Franklin, Tennessee. She stargazes on warm summer nights and occasionally indulges in afternoon tea.

Although, published in the Christian non-fiction market under her real name, Joy Griffin Dent, it was the empty nest that turned her to writing romantic fiction. Proving that it's never too late to follow your dreams.

Please follow Darcy on Twitter: @darcyflynn and Facebook: http:/www.facebook.com/DarcyFlynnAuthor and visit her website: www.darcyflynnromances.com, or feel free to drop her a line at: darcyflynnromances@gmail.com.

OTHER TITLES BY DARCY FLYNN:

9 781941 925133